THE GUARDIAN'S PATH

It's YOUR Call
with more than 20 possible endings

Disney **PRINCE OF**
PERSIA
THE SANDS OF TIME

THE
GUARDIAN'S
PATH

Written by Carla Jablonski
Based on the screenplay written by Doug Miro & Carlo Bernard
From a screen story by Jordan Mechner and Boaz Yakin
Executive Producers Mike Stenson, Chad Oman, John August, Jordan Mechner,
Patrick McCormick, Eric McLeod
Produced by Jerry Bruckheimer
Directed by Mike Newell

Disney PRESS
New York

Printed in the United States of America

First Edition

1 3 5 7 9 10 8 6 4 2

J689-1817-1-10060

Library of Congress Catalog Card Number on file.

ISBN 978-1-4231-2700-0

Visit www.disneybooks.com

In your hands you hold an object of great power. It has the ability to alter the course of history. The choices YOU make with this item will impact moments in time, fateful events, and could even mean the difference between life and death for those closest to you.

As Princess Tamina, will you fulfill your destiny and save the Dagger? OR will you become just another victim of the Persian Empire's reign? These, and countless other choices are yours to make. Will you find your path or will you be lost forever?

It's YOUR call.

Prologue

You were born with a sacred duty—a destiny. Like your ancestors, you have a responsibility so great there have been times you wondered if the burden was too much to bear. For you, Princess Tamina, are charged with protecting the very fabric of time—as a Guardian. You have been given the task of keeping the secrets of the Sandglass of Time safe and of protecting its mystical Dagger.

However, you fear now that all your beliefs are about to be tested. The barbaric Persians are outside the gates of your holy city of Alamut, putting the Dagger in danger. You hope you will be able to rise to this moment and live up to your destiny.

You stand in your chamber as your attendants paint you with sacred henna tattoos.

"Princess Tamina," a voice says.

You turn to see the Regent of Alamut, bearded and bent with age, standing in the doorway.

"Enter," you say. The Regent steps into your lush chamber. You don't like the serious expression on his face; it bodes trouble.

"The Persian army, my princess," he says. "It has not moved on. I fear—"

You cut him off. "Show me," you say.

 TURN TO PAGE 2

2

You walk briskly outside and out along the ramparts of Alamut's walls. The Regent and your bodyguards hurry to keep up. The stars glitter in the dark sky, but clouds cover the moon, making even these well-known walkways seem ominous.

Now you see other flickering lights—below you, on the ground. Fires from the Persian camp. They are preparing for an attack, you are certain.

"My princess," the Regent calls, "perhaps it would be safer if you didn't stand so close to the edge."

You clutch the rough stone, drumming your fingers. Their numbers are great; but your convictions are greater.

"Gather council," you tell the Regent. "Tell them I sit in the High Temple. I must pray." You turn from the rampart and head up a winding staircase.

The Regent follows behind you, confused. "The High Temple? Alamut hasn't been breached in a thousand years." He does not say it aloud but you know his concern—that the Persians will take the city and discover its secrets.

"Everything changes in time," you say, without breaking stride. "We should know this best of all."

TURN TO PAGE 3

The ornate High Temple sits above the city, nestled among the clouds. You spend the night in prayer with your retinue, seeking the strength and wisdom you'll need to face what's to come.

At dawn, an Alamutian soldier bursts into your sanctuary. "Persians have breached the eastern gates!" he cries.

All eyes turn to you. "Collapse the passages to the chamber," you order. "Go now, all of you." They file out of the temple, casting worried glances at you. Only a tall, elegant warrior stays behind. This is your trusted advisor, Asoka.

"Above all else," you say, repeating the words you've heard all your life, "it must be saved. Yes, Asoka?"

"Yes, Princess," Asoka says.

You kneel before an ornate column. You touch your forehead to the floor and stretch out your arms. You whisper the ancient words. There is a soft rumble, and a radiant light pours out of the column as it swings open.

You stand and step inside the revealed tabernacle. You take a glowing dagger from its resting place and wrap it in an embroidered cloth. It is more powerful than anyone might imagine.

The Dagger must be kept safe.

Should you give it to Asoka to take out of the city or should you do it yourself?

If you give it to Asoka to take to the Guardian Temple in the North, **TURN TO PAGE 10.**

If you believe you should take it yourself, **TURN TO PAGE 85.**

4

You and Dastan have been riding all day. Up ahead you see a welcome sight: an oasis! The lush greens and blues stand out in high relief against the sandy desert.

"Our journey is blessed," you say. "We'll stop for water, push for the mountain pass by nightfall."

"I think you're enjoying telling me what to do a little too much," Dastan complains, but he grins at you.

You grin back. You are finally heading in the right direction. You're glad you told him the truth.

The oasis is beautiful, full of tall grasses, wildflowers, and a rippling blue pool. Aksh drinks thirstily as you and Dastan fill the canteens. You hear a rustling sound and look up. Right into the face of a gawky ostrich. You stare at it. It stares at you.

As you try to understand what this means, Sheikh Amar and his armed men step out of the bushes. All of their weapons are drawn. The last time you saw this man, you ruined his ostrich-racing ring and caused a riot among his people.

Uh-oh.

"We parted under rushed circumstances," Amar says coldly. "We never got a chance to say good-bye."

 TURN TO PAGE 19

With the guard by your side, you make your way back to the palace. You grip the Dagger, the feel of the handle giving you courage.

Nizam gave you two days until the king's arrival. Maybe he won't suspect you accomplished your mission so quickly. You need to get out of the city before he knows you have the Dagger.

When you're alone, you slip out of the palace through one of the side entrances, desperately hoping that no one realizes it's you, as you are still in servant's clothes. You're going to need a horse, provisions . . . it's a long way to go to bring the Dagger to safety at the Guardian Temple in the north.

You duck into an alley to gather your thoughts. Three large men with weapons appear opposite you. "Just where do you think you're going, Princess?" one of them growls. How did they recognize you?

"We're to take you to Nizam," another one says. He had you followed! "And if you put up any argument, he has instructed us to relieve you of the Dagger in any way necessary. He intends to use it the moment the king arrives, and to see his plan through."

Nizam knew you had the Dagger. The guard must have seen Dastan give it to you and reported it to Nizam. Have you gotten the Dagger just to lose it again?

 TURN TO PAGE 8

6

That night you fall into a restless sleep. At dawn the next morning, you wake to find Dastan tearing a blanket into strips.

"What are you doing?" you ask.

He kneels down and wraps the fabric around Aksh's hooves. "Garsiv can't be far behind," he explains. "Aksh is the most famous horse in the empire. This will obscure his tracks."

"Tracks where?" you ask. "Where are you going?"

Dastan works quickly, anxious to get moving. "The holy city of Avrat, where Persian kings are buried. My uncle Nizam will be there for my father's funeral. He's the only one I can trust. He'll listen to me, see I was set up by Tus."

He climbs onto Aksh. You step in front of the horse.

"You're wanted for the king's *murder*," you say. "And you're going to march into his funeral, alongside thousands of Persian soldiers?"

"Step aside, Princess," Dastan says.

You stand your ground. "Every road to Avrat will be covered with Persian troops—"

"I'm not taking roads," Dastan says, cutting you off. "I'm going through the Valley of the Slaves."

You gape at him. "You've got to be joking! I've heard servants whispering of it. No one goes near that wasteland—it's filled with murdering cutthroats!"

"So they say." Dastan kicks the horse, and it brushes past you.

He's leaving you here? And taking the Dagger with him!

You have to stop him.

 TURN TO PAGE 107

Dastan looks as though he is about to say something when suddenly the valley fills with the sound of thundering hoofbeats.

The Persian cavalry bursts through the treeline. You and Dastan try to run, but you're quickly surrounded. Persian guards aim crossbows at you as you stand in front of the farmhouse.

Dastan's brother, Prince Garsiv, strides toward you.

"Garsiv, listen to me!" Dastan cries. "Nizam is the traitor! *He's* the one who poisoned Father's robe. He's after the crown! And he's brought back the Hassansins!"

Then you see the twisting sand funnels. "Oh, no," you say, breathing hard. "They're here."

Seven Hassansins charge toward you on powerful black stallions. Their chain-mail cloaks and terrifying array of weapons glint in the sun, making you squint. They will descend upon you in moments.

Do you stay and fight or do you use their arrival as a diversion to take the Dagger into the temple?

If you stay and fight, TURN TO PAGE 112.

If you sneak away to the temple,
TURN TO PAGE 41.

"What does Nizam want with the princess? And her dagger?" a voice behind you asks.

You turn to see Prince Dastan—and he's not alone. Several of his men are with him.

Without a word, Nizam's men take off running. You're not sure if they're afraid of fighting Dastan and his men or if they're off to warn Nizam that he's been exposed.

"What are you doing here?" you ask the prince.

"You got me thinking," he says. "Your worry seemed sincere. So I followed you, to see what you would do next. I'm sorry to say that you're right—Nizam is up to something. Not sure what or why—but if he's willing to kill you over a dagger and has a plan we know nothing of, well, perhaps we *shouldn't* trust him." He turns to his men. "Have Nizam brought to my brothers and I. We need to question him."

"Thank you," you say.

"So, tell me, what's so special about the Dagger?" he asks.

"Now, Prince," you tease, "allow a girl *some* secrets."

He gives you a puzzled but amused look. Perhaps when you return from bringing the Dagger to the Guardian Temple, you can get to know Prince Dastan better. And perhaps someday you will even tell him the story of the Dagger. Perhaps . . .

THE END

This is a dangerous, violent storm. You need to take cover fast. The caves are a lot closer than the city. You quickly guide Astrella into the nearest one. The storm has her very jumpy. You dismount and soothe her as best you can.

The rain pours down, and outside the hard ground is quickly turning into mud. Unfortunately so is the ground inside the cave. That's when you realize the cave is on lower ground than the path leading to it. Rain is quickly seeping in.

"Come on, Astrella," you say, taking her reins, "let's move farther back."

The sky is very dark as the storm worsens, making it nearly impossible to see inside the cave. You wish you had a lantern or even just a few matches. You hate how vulnerable you feel, not being able to see your surroundings. There could be bats, snakes, lizards, cobwebs, spiders, monsters, demons. . . .

TURN TO PAGE 72

10

"You know what must be done," you tell Asoka.

He takes the wrapped dagger from you and nods. You watch as he leaves, hoping you've made the right choice. You silently wish him a safe journey as you bring your veil down to cover your face.

You light the sweet incense, and the pungent smoke twists around you. You don't know how much time has passed when you hear heavy footsteps behind you.

"Silly songs and scented smoke will do little for you now," a gruff Persian soldier says. He knocks over an incense burner.

Cat quick, you kick up a knife concealed beneath the hearth and neatly catch it. Before you can use it, an older Persian with a bald head grabs your wrist.

"Perhaps there's a bit more to her than that, eh, Garsiv?" the older man says. He laughs and takes the knife from you.

Another Persian steps forward and uses the tip of his sword to move your veil aside. "So," he says, "for once the stories are true."

You glare at him, knowing he's referring to your reputation for being a beauty. As if something so superficial could matter in a time like this!

Now a young and handsome Persian soldier rushes into the room. Your eyes lock for a moment. He seems out of breath, as if he's been fighting. Of course they've all been fighting, you remind yourself. They've been fighting *your* people!

 TURN TO PAGE 53

The sky is illuminated with lightning flashes. You continue to walk through the maze of stalls, growing more and more puzzled and apprehensive. Could they have been abandoned because of a disease? A natural disaster? It's as if one day they all just walked away.

The skin on the back of your neck prickles. You can't see very well, but suddenly you have the sense that you aren't alone.

There's another resounding crash of thunder and explosion of lightning and you gasp. The lightning flash revealed someone hovering nearby. Watching you.

"Who are you?" you call. You don't want to get too close. You don't trust anyone who sneaks up on you, observes you silently.

"Why don't you answer?" you demand. You reach for the Dagger, prepared to defend yourself.

TURN TO PAGE 120

"What, pray tell, does Dastan have that your mistress would like returned?" Nizam asks.

"I'd like to know the same thing," a voice behind you says.

You whirl around to see Prince Dastan striding toward you. As he comes up beside you, he frowns.

"You say it is your mistress, the *princess*, who asks to find me? What is her message?" He is studying your face intently. Your stomach clenches. You have the terrible feeling that he knows who you really are.

You're not comfortable being questioned by both men. If things go wrong, you're outnumbered.

Now that you've found Dastan, there's no way to know if he'll actually agree to your request. Then you'll need to take it from him forcibly—and you don't want Nizam there to witness, or to stop you.

It might make sense to speak with Nizam privately and have him request the Dagger from Dastan, since Dastan is unlikely to deny him. But you don't know if Nizam can be persuaded.

Both men are waiting for you to say something. Which one should you try to meet with alone? And once you do, how will you get him to agree?

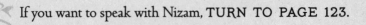

If you want to speak with Nizam, TURN TO PAGE 123.

If you want to speak with Prince Dastan,
TURN TO PAGE 126.

The storm is over. Dastan pulls back the makeshift tent, and you see that dawn has broken. As the rising sun crests over a dune, you pull out the amulet.

"The sands contained within the Sandglass are volatile," you say. "That's why it's a completely sealed system."

You hold up the amulet to the rising sun and whisper an incantation. You hear Dastan gasp beside you as the sunlight refracts through the amulet's crystal, forming into a three-dimensional hologram of a spinning globe.

"Opening the Dagger while it's in the chamber breaks the seal," you say.

Beautiful, majestic cities all over the world appear in the crystal.

"No one knows for certain," you continue, "but it could destroy the Sandglass. Cause it to crack and shatter."

Now an apocalyptic sandstorm appears to approach the spinning holographic cities. Quickly, the cities are covered with oceans of sand.

"All of mankind would pay for Nizam's lust for power," you say.

The hologram shows people fleeing, screaming in horror, choking to death, being buried alive as the sandstorm covers the planet.

The hologram fades and you gesture to the storm-blown sand around you. "This is all that would be left of us."

TURN TO PAGE 74

You lean in, as if to kiss him. Dastan seems transfixed, uncertain. Seizing your chance, you quickly reach for the Dagger.

Not quickly enough. Dastan smacks away your hand. You leap up and grab his sword from where it hangs on the horse's saddlebag. You swing it wildly. It is far heavier than you anticipated.

Dastan jumps back, barely escaping the sharp tip of the blade. He whistles, and the horse, responding to the signal, steps forward, banging into you. You slam into Dastan.

Your fingers grip the Dagger's handle and you yank it from his belt. *Ha! Got it!* you say to yourself.

But once again he's too fast for you. He flips you onto your back and you fall hard onto the ground. The Dagger goes flying.

You scramble after it, but Dastan gets to it first. He grabs it— and as he does his fingers hit the jewel on the Dagger. A trickle of sand releases into the air around him.

Oh, no! This is exactly what you were afraid of—that he would learn the secret of the Dagger.

But there's nothing you can do to stop it.

Or is there?

If you think it's too late, **TURN TO PAGE 79.**

If you try to get the Dagger away from Dastan, hoping to keep him from learning its secret, **TURN TO PAGE 43.**

With your hope gone, you follow Dastan's plan without question. All your faith is now in him. And he believes the Hassansins have returned the Dagger to Nizam in Alamut.

You arrive in the city just as dawn is breaking. You're horrified to see excavation sites everywhere. Nizam's desperation to find the Dagger and the Sandglass has destroyed your city.

And any minute now he may destroy all of humankind.

You must stop him!

"The Guardians built passageways underneath the city for secret access to the Sandglass," you tell Dastan.

Your eyes search for a specific carving on a nearby wall. You reach behind it and open a hidden door. You bring Dastan down a winding staircase and through the caverns that lead to the Sandglass. Suddenly, an earthquake shakes the tunnel.

"The digging is undermining the city!" Dastan gasps.

But you know better. "It's the gods. Nizam must have breached the Chamber of the Sandglass. He's almost there!"

You come to a room with a sand-covered floor. A golden cupola rises from the sand. Dastan starts to run toward it, but you grab his arm to stop him. "This is too dangerous," you tell him. "I must do this alone. You must get back aboveground."

"I'm coming with you," Dastan says.

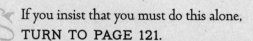

If you insist that you must do this alone,
TURN TO PAGE 121.

Or do you stop protesting and allow him to accompany you?
TURN TO PAGE 111.

Dastan gazes across the dunes. "I trusted him," he says, echoing your musings. "I thought he loved my father. But he didn't. He hated spending his life as brother to the king. He wanted the crown for himself."

He stands and paces as if the emotions churning inside him won't let him stay still. "But murdering my father. The Dagger. None of it makes him king." Dastan turns and looks at you. "What aren't you telling me?"

Your eyes travel from his tormented face to a terrifying sight behind him. A dark wall of sand is moving across the desert. A sandstorm. Coming right at you!

"We've got to move!" you cry.

"You know," he says, "you've got quick hands, but so do I." He holds up the Dagger. He must have taken it while you slept!

"If you want it back, tell me everything. No more games. No more lies!"

You stare at him, all too aware of the approaching sandstorm. Can you trust him with the truth?

 If you tell him everything, **TURN TO PAGE 93.**

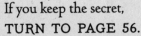 If you keep the secret,
TURN TO PAGE 56.

Y ou don't want to arouse suspicion—if you seek out Prince Dastan, you will draw attention to yourself, and perhaps to the Dagger. You will learn more by going through the motions of this distasteful ceremony.

There is a soft knock on the door. "Enter," you call.

"We are here to prepare you," a young Persian slave girl announces. You sigh and nod. They spend the next hour or so washing off your sacred henna tattoos and dressing you in elegant Persian finery. You don't speak, afraid your voice will betray your fear. You shut your eyes and take a deep breath, calming yourself.

You hear someone cough and your eyes flick open. Prince Dastan stands in the doorway, staring at you.

"I'm here to present you to the king, Your Highness," he says.

You shoo away the girls and stride out the door, forcing Prince Dastan to rush to catch up with you. You march down the corridor heading toward the great hall. You glance at his belt. Good. The Dagger is still there.

"So I'm escorted by Prince Dastan," you say, unable to push down the fury rising in you. "Must feel wonderful winning such acclaim for destroying an innocent city. Then again, you are a prince of Persia. Senseless and brutal."

He raises an eyebrow at you. "A pleasure to meet you, too," he says. "And allow me to offer that if punishing enemies of my king is a crime, it's one I'll gladly repeat."

You roll your eyes. "And he's thickheaded as well."

 TURN TO PAGE 62

You feel as if you've been riding for hours. You're not even very sure where you're going, other than that it's far away from the Valley of the Slaves. You figure once you're out of this narrow canyon, you'll stop to get your bearings.

First, though, you reach into your cloak and pull an ancient amulet from around your neck. You open it to see the pinch of glowing sand inside. You smile as you lift the Dagger so you can refill it. Suddenly, Aksh neighs.

You see five cloaked riders ahead of you!

You turn Aksh around, only to discover more riders. You're surrounded. Your eyes flash with determination as you leap from the horse. You draw Dastan's sword. But one of the riders seizes you. He is a large man with a shaved head and dark skin. His eyes are cold.

You struggle as a bearded, turbaned man approaches. He eyes you up and down, then calls over his shoulder, "You're right, she's not bad. We have a deal."

You're shocked to see one of the riders pull down his hood. Dastan!

"Glad to hear it, Sheikh Amar," the prince says. Then he strides to you and takes back the Dagger.

Your heart sinks. Not only does he have the Dagger again—he has *sold* you to these degenerates!

TURN TO PAGE 21

Sheikh Amar circles you. "The little riot you started kept going—for two days!" He gestures to the ostrich. "Bathsheba here is all that's left of my gambling empire! Look at the poor thing."

You blink at the ostrich. It blinks back.

"So it occurred to me the only way to recoup my tragic losses was to track down the young lovers who cast this dark cloud upon me. Yes, sir! I *need* the price on your heads!"

You blush at the word *lovers* and glance to see Dastan's reaction. But he doesn't seem to be paying attention. He's watching swirling funnels of sand dancing atop a sand dune. Another sandstorm?

Amar also looks to see what has Dastan transfixed. "Sand dervishes, Persian," he says dismissively. "As common as camel turds in this desert."

"Sheikh Amar, listen to me—" Dastan begins urgently.

Amar cuts him off. "I'd rather not." His men gag Dastan.

"Noble Sheikh," you say as respectfully as you can, "we are on a sacred journey."

Amar just rolls his eyes, and then you, too, are gagged. Worse, one of his men, a tall, bald, African named Seso, takes Dastan's sword—and your dagger.

TURN TO PAGE 84

You're not sure if you can get Astrella to climb that steep passageway, so you take the tunnel that leads deeper into the mountain. With the torchlight guiding you, she doesn't protest.

At first the tunnel is very narrow and you have to walk in front of Astrella. The walls are covered with a deep green moss, making it feel as if you're walking through a velvet corridor.

You hear the sound of water up ahead. Uh-oh. Is the rain coming in at the other end? But it doesn't sound like dripping or flooding. It reminds you of the calm lapping of gentle waves on a shore.

Could this path lead to an underground pool?

Your question is answered quickly. The narrow passageway widens, and soon you discover what looks like a lush valley hidden deep inside the mountain!

Wildflowers dot the hillside, and when you peer up you realize you are looking at sky. But not a rainy, dark, dismal sky. A clear, bright blue, glorious sky.

And then, you see the people!

TURN TO PAGE 130

After your hands are bound, you are led down a tunnel. You seethe beside Prince Dastan.

"Such a noble prince," you hiss at Dastan. "How taken you were by my fainting act. Eagerly leaping to assist the fallen beauty."

"Who said you were a beauty?" he retorts.

"There must be a reason you can't take your eyes off me," you taunt.

"I don't trust you. And don't worry, you're not my type."

"Of course! I'm not some desperate slave girl. I'm actually capable of voicing my own thoughts!"

"Too many for my taste," Dastan says.

Up ahead you can hear shouts and the rumble of a large crowd. Where are they taking you?

Sheikh Amar turns and grins at you. "The girl will make a nice addition," he says.

"What do you intend to do with her?" Dastan asks.

"Yes, do tell him," you sneer. "Can't you see how concerned he is?"

"Give me a moment with her," Dastan says, grabbing your arm.

Is he going to come up with a plan to get you out of here? Does he regret what he's done?

TURN TO PAGE 80

You have to get that dagger back! You dash onto the racetrack, which throws the ostriches into a panic. They squawk and screech, running this way and that. Men pour onto the track, trying to regain order, while others start fighting. You struggle to get to the man with your dagger, but by the time you arrive at the spot where you last saw him, he's gone.

Your head whips back and forth as you frantically search for him.

Someone roughly grabs your arm. "You!" Sheikh Amar shouts at you. "You did this!"

As his men get the riot under control, Amar drags you off the track. He shoves you in front of a tiny old woman sitting at a table.

"This one," he says to the woman. "You can have her. Cheap."

The wrinkled old creature looks you up and down. "She'll do. You're not allergic to camels, are you?"

"I—I don't think so," you say.

"Good." Turns out, the woman is a camel dealer, with a stable out in the middle of nowhere. She needs you to keep them in market condition.

Just great. The Dagger is gone, and now it appears you are destined to end your days as a camel beautician.

THE END

You need to help catch Prince Dastan—you can't risk his getting away with the Dagger. That could mean losing track of it forever.

You spot a window—and it looks as if that's where Dastan is heading. You race to it, and as Dastan rushes toward you, you fling yourself at his knees, knocking him over. You land together, arms and legs tangled.

Guards instantly surround you, and Garsiv binds Dastan's wrists. "I couldn't let a murderer escape," you explain as the uncle, Nizam, helps you up.

Nizam gives you a slight bow. "And for that we are grateful," he says. "So grateful, you should be rewarded."

Excellent. This is going exactly according to plan.

"The Dagger the murderous prince has in his possession is a sacred object to my people," you say. "I would be most grateful if you would return it to me."

Nizam's eyes narrow. "I am sorry. Giving a captive princess a dagger wouldn't be wise. Sacred or not, it is still a weapon. But I am sure Tus would be delighted to make you his wife—as now the king's choice for you is no longer available." He nods to the guards who haul Dastan away.

Your heart sinks. Marriage to Tus seems as cruel as Dastan's imprisonment. And you have no idea what will happen to the Dagger now. But you will spend the rest of your life searching for it.

THE END

24

The room grows silent. Prince Dastan gapes at you. Perhaps you should not have been so stubborn and taken greater care with your words. Luckily, the king seems more amused than offended.

"Clearly she will make a fine queen," he says. His eyes narrow as he studies you. "But Tus already has enough wives. You might take fewer chances, Dastan, if such a jewel waited in your chambers. The princess of Alamut will be your first wife." He grins at Prince Dastan. "What say you, Dastan?"

Now it's your turn to stare. This is a surprise. Dastan seems equally flabbergasted.

The king points at Dastan. "He plunges into a hundred foes without thought, but before marriage he stands frozen with fear."

The king laughs, and the crowd joins in heartily. Then his expression turns to panic. "The robe!" he screams. "It burns!"

You watch as several attendants pull at the robe, but they can't pry it off the king's body. Garsiv pushes through the crowd and rips at the robe. "My fingers!" he cries. He stumbles backward, clutching his hands.

"God help us," Nizam says, "the robe is poisoned." He whirls and points at Dastan. "The robe *Dastan* gave him!"

TURN TO PAGE 98

Dastan notices you hovering at the edge of the group. It distracts him, and his opponent gets in another hit.

"He favors his left!" you shout at Dastan. "And anticipates high!"

Dastan blinks, obviously surprised that you're yelling fighting advice at him. Then he whirls around and brings the club low and to the right. The other fighter drops to his knees. A cheer goes up. Thanks to you, Dastan has won.

You wait as he shakes hands with his opponent and returns the clubs to the men who lent them to him. He approaches you with a quizzical look.

"Did you decide to give me *Princess Tamina*'s message after all?" he asks with a teasing grin. "Or are you here to give me fighting pointers?"

You're not sure how to proceed. Is he more likely to give you the Dagger if you reveal Nizam's plotting? And if you do get the Dagger from the prince some other way, how are you going to keep it away from Nizam, and save your own life?

If you decide to tell him about Nizam,
TURN TO PAGE 87.

If you decide to keep quiet about that, and just ask for the Dagger, TURN TO PAGE 27.

Y ou need to get out of your chamber, fast. The royal family could arrive and marry you off to Prince Tus any moment! And then what would happen to the Dagger?

Luckily they have allowed one of your loyal maidservants to stay with you. Quickly, you exchange clothing with her, leaving her sitting with her back to the doorway. Anyone peeking in will believe you're sitting in quiet contemplation at your dressing table.

You cross to an intricately carved decorative platter mounted on the wall. You press the jeweled eye of a bird, the raised paw of a cat, and the rough bark of a tree and step back. The wall slides open, revealing a secret passageway. You step inside and press the same buttons on the inner wall. The door slides shut again. Did the Persians really believe you wouldn't know the palace's *many* secrets?

You welcome the cool quiet of the hidden room. You need this moment to think, to get your bearings. You must find Prince Dastan and somehow retrieve the Dagger.

You've heard from your maidservant that Prince Dastan often carouses with his men and almost seems more comfortable among common people than with royals. But his father, the king, is due to arrive at any moment. He could be staying close to his brothers right now. What should you do?

If you take to the streets, TURN TO PAGE 68.

If you search the palace compound,
TURN TO PAGE 95.

"Prince, you have something of mine that I'd like returned," you say calmly. "My dagger."

"Actually, Princess, I think *you* need to be returned. To your chambers," Dastan says. "You are to marry my brother to create an alliance between our peoples. We can't have you running around dressed as a servant. Who knows what trouble you may cause." He gives you a warning look. "And there *will* be trouble if you try to escape."

He gestures, and the crowd of men who had been watching the fight now surround you. "Let's escort the princess back to where she belongs," he says.

A messenger arrives on horseback. "Prince Dastan! I've been sent to find you," he says. "Your father, the king, has arrived!"

Prince Dastan's face lights up. "So soon!" He turns to you. "Let's dispense with formalities and introduce you right away."

The guards drag you to where the royal procession is arriving. You frantically try to think of a way to get the Dagger and to escape this terrible fate.

TURN TO PAGE 88

"Sorry, Princess," Prince Dastan says with a smirk. "You can't have your city back. It's in Persia's hands now."

You fight back your fury. Such insolence. But to snipe at him won't get you what you need. "I simply ask for you to return the Dagger you wear in your belt," you say softly. You can't risk the guard hearing.

He pulls it from his belt and holds it up. The jewel in the handle glints in the light. "Why should I?"

Your mind races. What will appeal to his pride? "You wouldn't have won that fight without my guidance," you remind him. "Surely you agree a gift of gratitude is in order."

His eyes narrow as he looks from the Dagger to you and then back again. Then he shrugs. "Why not?" He tosses the Dagger to you. You catch it neatly.

"Thank you," you say. You turn to go but feel you need to try one last time. After all, Dastan is not *all* that bad. "Please, Dastan. Keep a close eye on your uncle."

"That's an old trick, Princess," Dastan says. "Divide and conquer. You seek to create a rift in my family. It won't work."

You know not to say anything else. He could change his mind about the Dagger, and you can't risk that.

 TURN TO PAGE 5

"I can't help you!" you cry. "Leave me alone!"

They lunge at you and you scream. Then you realize—all you feel is a strange fluttering. They have passed right through you!

"Use the Dagger!" they cry. "Use the Dagger and bring us back to the time when we lived."

"I can't," you say. "That's not what it's for!"

You feel the odd sensation again as they try to get the Dagger away from you. Try as they might, though, they can't grasp the weapon. Their transparent fingers can't hold it.

"Get away from me!" you shout.

"Never," the voices moan. "We will never stop!"

Now you understand why the city was abandoned. The inhabitants must have discovered it was haunted!

You race to Astrella. Storm or no storm, you're getting out of there. Now!

TURN TO PAGE 99

You slip the Dagger from the secret pocket in your skirt and hold it out to her. Her eyes glitter as she takes it.

The moment it is in her hands, she laughs.

A terrible, horrible, evil laugh.

"Well done!" she shrieks. "Thank you for bringing it right to me!"

You stare speechlessly as the girl transforms in front of you. Her fingers become talons, and she grows much taller. Her teeth turn into fangs, and her face stretches and twists into a grotesque mask. Her skin grows mottled, until you realize it's not skin at all, but scales.

She's a demon!

You scream and turn to run but the demon's too quick. It's disgusting tongue flicks out and catches you, the way a frog might catch a fly!

As the demon pulls you closer and closer, its stinking breath makes your eyes tear. You struggle to escape, but it's impossible. Not only did you hand over the sacred Dagger to the evil creature, now you're going to be its dinner!

After being so easily duped, perhaps it's only right that this should be your . . .

END.

Your mind reels.

You're about to start begging, pleading, weeping even, if that's what it's going to take. But before you can say a word, Dastan puts a hand on your shoulder.

"I'm coming with you," he says. He climbs back up onto Aksh.

You watch him, confused. "You—you're going to help me?"

Dastan gazes down at you. You can see something has changed deep within him. He reaches out his hand to you. "We can sit here and chat, or you can get on the horse."

You smile and take his hand.

TURN TO PAGE 4

"Dastan, if you give me that dagger I can give you anything you want. Your heart's desire. Riches beyond your imagining," you say.

"Not interested," he says.

"How can you say that?" you ask. "Everyone has something they want. I promise you, I can provide it. Do you want a palace? A harem of beautiful women? Armor of the finest materials?"

You watch as Dastan does something strange. He takes off his shirt and wraps it around his head, covering his ears. "What are you doing?" you ask.

He points at his ears and shrugs. Now you understand. He doesn't want to listen to you!

You fall behind a bit as you try to come up with a new plan. Suddenly a searing pain shoots up your leg. You glance down to see a scorpion scurry away. You've been stung!

"Dastan!" you cry. "Help!"

But he just keeps walking. He can't hear you!

"Dastan, please. . . ." you try again. But it's no use.

He gets further and further away as you call out, growing weaker by the minute. Your mission has been a failure in . . .

THE END.

The man's words barely register. Your mind is reeling.

"Tamina," Dastan says urgently, "if Nizam knows of this place we have to get out of here."

You stand up and push past him without a word. You have no time to mourn—you know what you must do. "There's only one way to stop all this," you declare. "To be sure the Dagger is safe."

"How?" Dastan asks.

Can you tell him? You decide you must.

"The temple holds the stone the Dagger came from," you say. "The first thing we learn, if all else fails—put the Dagger back in the stone. The stone will envelop it, pull it into the mountain. The Dagger will disappear forever, returning to the gods." You feel dazed, as the implications of what you're about to do rush into your thoughts.

Dastan must notice the gravity of your expression. "What else? Tell me, Tamina!"

You take a deep breath. "The original promise must be fulfilled."

Dastan takes a step backward as if your words have knocked him off-balance. "The girl who offered her life for mankind," he says slowly. "You plan to take her place. You'll die!"

"The gods must take back the life they spared," you reply simply.

TURN TO PAGE 7

Hours later you are seated behind Dastan on the great warhorse Aksh riding alongside a river. You are miles away from Alamut. Dastan signals the horse to stop and you both dismount. Dastan kneels beside the river, letting the water drip through his fingers.

"This stream is a tributary of the river that runs through Avrat," he says sadly. "The water they'll use to wash his body."

At first you find his words perplexing, then you realize he's speaking of his father. "You mourn the father you murdered?" you ask.

He glares at you. "I did not murder my father."

You nod, surprised by how quickly you believe him. But if not Dastan, who poisoned the robe? You sit beside him.

"It was foolish of you to add my troubles to your own," he says.

You remember the moment you discovered that he had the Dagger. It was when Tus threatened your life. He pulled it out—as if he meant to defend you, even against his own family.

"You were ready to risk everything for me," you say. "I saw that in your eyes."

"I swore to my brother I'd take your life, rather than let any other have you," he confesses.

Interesting, you think.

TURN TO PAGE 14

Dastan begins pacing, tossing the Dagger from one hand to the other. You're not sure what has him so agitated. He is muttering to himself, but loudly enough for you to hear.

"After the battle, he asked for this Dagger as tribute. I didn't think anything of it. It was Tus!" Dastan turns to face you, his eyes cold. "*He* gave me the gift that killed our father. He stands to be crowned king. With this Dagger he could change course at a critical moment of a battle, foresee the blade of a rival. He'd be invincible." Now he gazes up at the stars. "Tus is behind it all. My *brother*."

You don't know what to say to him. You can see it's as if his world is collapsing. You feel a pang of sympathy. But that doesn't change things. In fact, now that he knows about the Dagger's power, Dastan is much more dangerous to you—whether or not he is hurting.

TURN TO PAGE 6

You don't want to risk joining up with strangers. You duck behind a dune and wait for them to pass. Then you continue making your way across the harsh and unforgiving landscape.

You have the awful sense that you're being followed. But any time you turn, all you see are swirling dust funnels.

You have to take a break. You find a scraggly tree and drop under it, grateful for the small patch of shade. The heat must be affecting you—it looks as if there are furrows forming under the sand. Heading straight toward you.

You shriek as a pit viper bursts out of the sand. Then another! And another!

Then three dark-cloaked men thunder toward you, riding massive horses. Why didn't you hear them? What is going on?

"Stay back!" you shout. You grip the Dagger. Should you use it to turn back time?

Before you can decide, the vipers strike! One sinks its fangs deep into your hand, making you drop the Dagger. You fall to the ground and watch, amazed, as another snake swoops in and picks up the Dagger in its mouth. It slithers up the leg of one of the men, who pockets the weapon with a smile.

"Thank you, Princess Tamina," the man says. "We've been searching for this."

Without another word, they turn the horses around and vanish beyond the horizon. The snakes disappear, too. Who *are* they? you wonder. How did they find you?

You'll never know. The viper's venom soon takes over your body. This is your . . .

END.

"I mean no disrespect," you say, "But the Dagger is entrusted to me, and I must keep it in my possession until I get to my destination."

She smiles. "Well said. I am proud that you are a Guardian. The Dagger of Time and its secrets are well protected. I can see that."

"Thank you," you say, relieved she isn't offended.

"I know you must have questions," she says, "but now is not the time. We will meet again one day."

You're disappointed that you can't spend more time with her, but she's right. The Dagger must be brought to safety.

You lead Astrella back down the tiled passage. But when you turn to look back, the chamber has vanished. In fact, you realize, so has all the tile.

You reach the mouth of the cave and to your great surprise, find your trusted advisor, Asoka, waiting outside.

"What are you doing here?" you ask, rushing to greet him.

"Good news, Princess," Asoka says. "The Persians have left the city! I don't know why—but you may return with the Dagger. All is well."

"That's wonderful!" you say. "But how did you ever find me?"

"I'm not really sure," Asoka says. "I felt guided by some kind of *intuition*."

You have a feeling there were other hands at work in ridding Alamut of the Persians and in bringing Asoka to you.

"Thank you," you whisper toward the cave. Then you mount Astrella and you and Asoka head home.

THE END

Both you and Prince Dastan could be recognized by the many dignitaries arriving for the king's funeral. You can't risk that.

You scan the area and notice a small trapdoor just around the side of the entrance into the city. "Let's go see where that leads," you suggest. "It could be the water system."

Dastan nods. "If we travel underground, we'll be hidden."

You slip through the masses of people and make your way over to the trapdoor. With all eyes on the procession, no one notices Dastan yank the iron ring and pull the trapdoor open. You quickly climb down the steel rungs, and he pulls the door closed behind him.

That's when you notice something—the stench!

"Bad idea," you choke out.

Dastan pushes up on the trapdoor but it doesn't budge. "There must be something blocking it now. A horse, or a carriage, maybe." He turns back to look at you. "We must be in the sewer system."

You nod, covering your nose. "Well, it will still get us inside the city," you say, trying not to inhale. "Even if it is disgusting."

You start down the maze of tunnels. Unfortunately, it's not just repulsive—it's also really confusing. You get hopelessly lost.

This just might be where you and Dastan spend the rest of your lives. It is just the beginning of . . .

THE END.

Shaking your head, you urge Astrella into a gallop and soon catch up with Kartosh. "Never would have guessed that a mud horse could move so quickly," you comment.

"There's a lot you don't know," Kartosh says. "And much I'd like to know about you."

You want to avoid his questions, so you decide to ask your own. "Why were you in the box?" you ask.

"A minor disagreement," the genie says. "I am grateful that you broke the spell."

"I did?" you say, perplexed. "How?"

"First, by opening the box. That's how I knew that you have a sacred destiny. You are human, that's easy to see. But only a very special human would be able to get the latch to release. And then, by inviting me to join you."

"What do you mean?" you ask.

"The spell would only be lifted if I was invited to leave the cave."

So that's why he made you ask him again. You want to ask who put him in the box when you notice Astrella has grown agitated. She keeps looking back. So you glance over your shoulder.

"Uh-oh," you say. "A sandstorm!" Sand funnels in the distance twist toward you. Strange—the funnels are moving completely in synch.

Kartosh looks back. "That's not a sandstorm," he says. Then he looks at you. "It appears, traveler, you have very powerful enemies."

 TURN TO PAGE 66

For the first few miles you stay off the roads completely—you don't want the Persian army to stop you. Eventually the terrain turns rougher, and you begin to feel fairly safe.

Safe from the Persians, at least. You still have no idea what to expect as you head farther and farther away from Alamut. You've never left the city walls before. You've never had a reason to.

No matter. You have the memory of every lesson you ever had as a Guardian to guide you. That is security enough.

You feel even more reassured when a city looms up ahead, precisely where it was foretold in the legends. And, just as in the directions you recited again and again, there are caves carved into the sheer rock face to your right. Perfect. You're exactly where you should be.

Strange, you think, as you get closer to the city it looks abandoned. The walls are in disrepair and the crumbling gates are wide open. Then again, the stories of the journey to the temple have come down from ages long past. It could have been a bustling market city a thousand years ago!

The sky darkens and lightning flashes across the sky. You need to take cover. Should you hurry to the city and find shelter in one of the buildings? Or should you duck into one of the nearby caves and wait out the weather?

If you want to seek shelter in a cave, TURN TO PAGE 9.

If you'd rather get to the city,
TURN TO PAGE 91.

You know your duty. You have to protect the Dagger. Return it to the temple. In the chaos of the fight you sneak away and climb up onto the farmhouse roof. Your eyes scan the rock face. There is the entrance to the cave!

If you didn't know to look for it, you'd never find it. At least, that's what you hope. You slip into the fissure in the rock and enter the cave that is the temple.

Light reflects off a natural pool. You can no longer hear the battle outside. Your thoughts flash to Dastan—you hope he's safe. But then you bring your focus back to this moment. You need all your will and strength to take the next steps.

You see the sacred mantle of rock at the back of the pool. This is where you will fulfill your destiny. Where you will give your life to save humankind.

You wade into the water, just as your ancestor did years before you.

"There's another way," Dastan says behind you. You turn to face him, relieved that he survived the battle outside.

"There isn't. I'm ready for this," you say. You lift the Dagger, preparing to thrust the blade into the sacred stone. Saving humanity but ending your life.

Vhwip! A whip suddenly wraps around your wrist and yanks you away from the stone! The Dagger goes flying, and you slam your head against a boulder.

Darkness envelops you as you pass out.

 TURN TO PAGE 113

Hoping to find something useful, you twist the jar lid and are very glad you opened it. Inside is a torch and matches! It takes a few tries but you manage to light the torch.

Now you can see the cave much better. No bats, no monsters. Just jagged rock walls, muddy ground, and dank smells. The torch casts spooky shadows, but it's better than standing there in the dark.

Astrella whinnies and picks up her hooves daintily, as if she is disturbed by the mud underfoot. The water is still flowing into the cave. You need to go even deeper. You hold up the torch and are able to see that at the back of the cave there are tunnels—one leading steeply up and perhaps out, the other leading deeper into the mountain.

Which should you and Astrella take?

 Take the one that leads up, TURN TO PAGE 108.

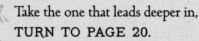 Take the one that leads deeper in, TURN TO PAGE 20.

You can't let him discover the secret of the Dagger. There is only one hope—only the one holding the Dagger is aware of what it can do. You *must* be sure he isn't holding it!

With a shriek you fling yourself at Dastan, startling him. He drops the Dagger into the river.

You plunge into the river after it. You have no idea what happens if no one holds the Dagger as the sands release—and you don't want to find out. And you can't lose it, not after just getting it back!

Time and again, you duck below the surface, trying to find the Dagger. Your wet clothes weigh you down. Each time you surface, it gets a little harder. You keep repeating and repeating the action over, and over, again.

Gradually, all your strength runs out of you. You slip under, and this time you can't fight it. This is . . .

THE END.

44

Scanning the crowds, you see Dastan sitting with Sheikh Amar. They are talking excitedly, and you glare at the prince. But then something changes between them; what had been friendly has become charged. To your horror you see Seso take the Dagger from Dastan! He gives it to Amar. Amar tosses it to someone down on the racetrack. "Melt it down for the jewels," you hear Amar instruct the man.

You can't let that happen!

But what should you do?

Should you create a diversion so that Dastan can get the Dagger? Or should you go after the man who has it yourself?

If Dastan gets the Dagger back, you'll still have to get it back from him!

But Dastan is in a better position to stop the man.

If you go for the man yourself, **TURN TO PAGE 22.**

If you create a diversion,
TURN TO PAGE 71.

You've been walking for what seems like miles. You wish you'd taken the time to find shoes that fit properly—the large size of the ones you're wearing makes you clumsy, and you can feel blisters rising. The good thing is that your disguise appears to be working. No one pays any attention to a slim young man wearing worker's clothes and a turban, which also hides your hair.

Finally you've reached the right quarter—or at least you think it's the right one. The streets are jumbled close together, and clusters of men gather on the corners. Some of them are quite boisterous, others argumentative. There is the distinct odor of ale mixed with sweat and dust. All seem at leisure. You wrinkle your nose, reluctant to approach any of them to ask about Dastan. You have a feeling that your disguise may no longer work the minute you speak. You forgot about that detail.

Then you spot some men you recognize as the prince's bodyguards!

They are piling out of a tavern and into an alley. You follow along, figuring you'll at least get word of Prince Dastan's whereabouts from this crowd.

Then your eyes grow wide. Destiny *must* be at work! Prince Dastan has just sauntered out of the tavern after his men.

But *what* is he doing?

TURN TO PAGE 124

The plaza is quiet—much quieter than it would have been in a time of peace. Your own people are prisoners now, and the Persians occupying the city are soldiers. Most are in encampments outside the city walls. Perhaps this was the wrong place to look.

You hurry through the empty space, wondering where you should try next.

"Stop right there!" a voice calls out.

You turn slowly. You recognize the man—he is Nizam, the king's brother and the princes' uncle.

"On whose business do you wander the palace, girl?" he demands.

No business of yours, you want to say, but hold your tongue. You remember that you are dressed in your maidservant's clothing.

You bow your head. "I was asked to find the young prince. Dastan, I believe is his name?"

He peers at you with suspicion. "On whose order? And for what reason?"

Hmm. You hadn't thought that far.

Perhaps you should tell him something close to the truth—after all, he doesn't know the secret of the Dagger.

"The princess Tamina believes the prince has something belonging to her. She asked me to beg him to return it. Or," you add, thinking fast, "to do her the honor of returning it out of kindness as a wedding gift. Since she is to marry his brother."

Nizam's eyes narrow. Have you said too much?

TURN TO PAGE 12

"You know, you really walk like one," you comment after a while.

Dastan keeps going.

"Head held high, chest out. Long stomping strides. The walk of a self-satisfied Persian prince. No doubt it comes from being told the world is yours since birth. And actually believing it."

Dastan whirls around. "I wasn't born in a palace like you," he says. "I was born in the slums of Nasaf. I lived if I fought or clawed for it."

You stare at him, stunned. You had no idea. "Then how . . . ?"

"The king rode into the market one day and found me. Took me in. Gave me a life. A family. A home. So what you're looking at is the walk of a man who just lost everything."

He turns back around and starts walking again. You stand gazing at him. This Prince Dastan is turning out to be very surprising.

TURN TO PAGE 118

48

"Then we have an agreement," Nizam says, leaning in close. You can see every pore on his face, every eyelash.

"Yes," you croak.

"Good." He releases you, and you rub your throat. "Remember—I am not as foolish, gullible, or headstrong as any of my nephews. I will be much harder to betray. And I know not to trust you."

"I feel the same way about you," you say. "So how do you expect me to get the Dagger from Dastan? Why can't *you* just ask him for it?"

"Too direct," Nizam says. "Right now they believe it's a trinket of yours. None of them know what power it truly represents."

You swallow hard. *He knows!* He knows *everything*. How is that possible? This is *much* worse—and far more dangerous—than you had realized. Nizam will fight to the death to get the Dagger, that you know for sure. And he will kill any who stand in his way.

TURN TO PAGE 51

"I believe in what I can hold in my fist and see with my eyes," Dastan says.

"Then you limit your sight," you counter. "Miss your sacred calling."

"Spend time hungry and cold in the gutter. Then talk to me about sacred callings."

"I know what the gods have asked of me," you say. "And I've dedicated my life to it. I will fulfill that calling, no matter what the consequences."

You let your words sink in. You need him to see that the Dagger is part of something far greater than clearing his name, wealth, or power.

"I'm begging you," you continue. "Stop thinking about what you lost, what you used to be. And start thinking: what are you supposed to *become*?"

Dastan remains silent. You think you may have struck a chord.

"I suspect it's greater than marching into this funeral and getting your head chopped off," you finish.

He faces you square on. "Destiny or not, if you want to stay close to your precious dagger, you're going to help me get into Avrat."

You sigh. You have no choice. You have to help him sneak into the city.

Do you hire on with one of the dignitaries to get into the city? TURN TO PAGE 67.

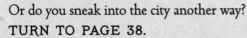

Or do you sneak into the city another way?
TURN TO PAGE 38.

"I'm desperate for a drop of water," you call. "This canteen is empty!"

"Perhaps you should have thought ahead, Princess," Dastan scolds. "Rather than using up all of the water."

"I wasn't born of this desert like you Persians," you retort. "My constitution is more delicate."

"I think you mean spoiled," Dastan counters.

Okay, time to put your plan into action. You fall to the ground and wait.

"A miracle," Dastan calls over his shoulder. "I've silenced the princess."

Steady, you tell yourself. He should turn around just about—

"Tamina!" he cries.

He rushes to your side and kneels down beside you. He turns to get the canteen from Aksh's saddle, and as he does, you slam his head with a bone you've picked up. He stares at you a moment, then flops over. He's out cold.

You quickly pull the Dagger from his belt and mount Aksh.

"Yee-hah!" you cry as Aksh takes off at a gallop.

 TURN TO PAGE 18

"How do you want me to proceed?" you ask.

Nizam gives you a cool smile. "You're a smart girl. You'll think of something. You have two days. That's when the king is due to arrive."

You blink as he stands. "Two days?" you repeat. "That's not enough time!"

"Dastan has probably made his way just outside the city walls," he says, then strides away. "I suggest you start there."

You sit staring into space for a moment, but fury very quickly replaces your sense of fear and helplessness. Not only are you going to get the Dagger back, you vow, but you are going to expose Nizam's treachery. You have no doubt that his plans for the Dagger don't include the rest of the royal family. In fact, you suspect it threatens them.

But how can you convey that to Prince Dastan and still manage to keep the Dagger and its secrets? What if Nizam does tell the royal family about the power of the Dagger? They'll certainly want it for themselves.

You'll worry about all that later. Now you have to find Dastan—and hope that he will help you. Together you need to come up with a plan.

TURN TO PAGE 101

52

You gallop for what feels like forever, the moonlight showing you the way. "It's safe to stop now, Persian," Amar finally calls.

"They won't stop," Dastan replies. "They track and kill. That's what they do."

"What *who* do?" Amar asks. You're wondering the same thing.

Dastan stops the horse and nervously looks back the way you came. "Those vipers who attacked us in the camp were controlled. By a dark secret of the empire—Hassansins."

You shudder. You've heard tales, but thought they were just stories told to frighten people.

"For years they were the covert killing force of Persian kings," Dastan continues. "But my father ordered them disbanded. Nizam must have secretly kept the Hassansins intact. They are no ordinary soldiers, but a cult of killers trained from childhood. They'll do Nizam's bidding without question."

You see Seso and Amar's fear as they understand fully who is following you.

"This is why we can't stop," Dastan says.

Silently, and with grim expressions, you all begin riding again. It seems you now have a much larger party accompanying you and the Dagger to the Guardian Temple.

TURN TO PAGE 89

You jerk your head sharply, and your veil falls back into place.

The older man paces in front of you. "We know you secretly build weapons for enemies of Persia," he says. "Now show us where."

"We have no secret forges here, and what weapons we do have, you can easily overcome," you tell him.

"Our spies say differently, Princess," the one called Garsiv snarls. "Much pain can be spared if you—"

You cut him off. "All the pain in the world won't help you find something that doesn't exist."

Now the one who lifted your veil approaches you. "Spoken like one wise enough to consider a political solution, don't you think, Nizam?"

The older man shrugs. "Perhaps, Tus," he says.

Tus extends his hand to you. "Join hands with Persia's future king."

You sneer. *This* is the crown prince? "I'll die first."

You see Tus's jaw clench. "Yes," he says softly. "Yes you will."

Your heart clutches as he steps back and motions to his bodyguard, who draws his sword. The young and handsome Persian reaches for his belt. He lifts a dagger as if he intends to defend you—against his own people! But more shocking—

He's holding *your* sacred dagger! Asoka has failed.

"Wait!" you cry.

TURN TO PAGE 125

"I'm sorry," you tell Kartosh. "I travel alone. Now please, get out of the way." You slip your hand into your skirt pocket, touching the Dagger. If you have to, you'll fight your way out.

"It has been nearly a thousand years since anyone opened the box," Kartosh says. The genie is expanding before your eyes. "I will *not* go back to a life in exile."

You pull out the Dagger, but before you can attack he lets out a deafening roar. The cave shakes and rocks and boulders begin dropping around you. Astrella lets out a terrified whinny.

"Stop it!" you scream at Kartosh. But he keeps up his howl. With horror, you realize the entrance to the cave has filled up with fallen rocks.

"No!" you cry. "All right, you can come with me!"

"Too late," the genie says. "The way is blocked. Oh, and that magical knife you think you've hidden so well from me? It doesn't work on my kind. And now, I suggest you get comfortable. We have a lifetime to get to know each other."

THE END

Hours later, you and Dastan are walking to give Aksh a rest. The heat is blistering. You trail behind the prince, trying to come up with a way to get the Dagger back before you wind up in the Valley of the Slaves.

You watch, amused, as Dastan scoops up a handful of sand and refills the handle of the Dagger. "Without the right sand, it's just another knife," you point out. "Not even very sharp."

Dastan presses the jewels. Nothing happens.

"This sand," he says, "you have more of it?"

"Of course not," you tell him.

"How can I get some?"

"Try standing on your head and holding your breath."

You can't help it. You're enjoying his frustration.

"Keep walking," he snaps.

"I'm thirsty," you complain.

Dastan tosses you a canteen. You take a sip. "So if you can't show your uncle how the Dagger works, why in the world would he believe you?" you ask.

"That's not your problem, Princess," Dastan says.

You walk in uncomfortable silence for some time.

 TURN TO PAGE 47

You have vowed to keep this secret, and you can't break it now. But you still aren't sure you can trust Dastan—especially with something this huge, this important.

"Tell me, Princess!" he demands again.

"I . . . well . . . let's see . . . where should I begin . . ." you stammer, stalling, trying to come up with another story to give him. A lie.

Unfortunately, you wait too long. Within moments the raging sandstorm sweeps over you both. Burying you—and your secrets—forever.

THE END

Dastan is so startled he drops the Dagger. It skitters across the floor, and you lunge for it. Before you can reach it, he knocks you to the ground and pins you.

"What is going on here?" You turn your head to see the doorway filled with guards—and Prince Dastan's brother, Tus. He is glaring at you both.

"Thank goodness you stopped him!" you cry. Dastan quickly gets up, and you curl into a little ball to look helpless.

"She attacked me!" Dastan protests. "For this dagger." He picks it up, and you resist grabbing it again.

Instead, you push yourself up into a kneeling position and make yourself seem as pathetic as possible. "This man stole that dagger from one of my maidservants. He made her believe he loved her—just to steal this family heirloom. I was pleading with him to give it back. I must have said something wrong, for he suddenly attacked me!"

"She's lying," Dastan scoffs. "You don't believe her, do you?"

Tus's eyes are narrow as he studies Dastan. "First you disobey a direct order and launch a sneak attack without my knowledge or consent. Then I find you brawling with my bride-to-be. I believe *her* over you."

Dastan gapes at Tus. "Ask Nizam! She purposely sought me out."

"To beg for the Dagger for my maidservant," you explain, your voice quavering as you fake tears. "Her family has disowned her because of this incident."

"Give the knife to the girl," Tus orders. "Now."

 TURN TO PAGE 116

A short while later you are wishing you had taken Dastan's horse along with the Dagger. You stand and gaze at the desert in front of you. This is going to take forever! And you have no supplies. Perhaps you should have thought this through a little more.

No matter. You have a responsibility, a promise that you must keep. That's all that counts. Not your thirst, your fear, your exhaustion. Just the safety of the Dagger.

You twist up your long hair to get it off your neck and wipe away the sweat before it drips into your eyes.

You notice a Bedouin caravan cresting a nearby dune. Perhaps you should join them. They could provide you with protection, supplies, and even transport.

But you're not sure if you can really trust other people at this point. Not after everything you've been through.

 If you want to join the Bedouins, **TURN TO PAGE 77.**

If you want to continue on your own,
TURN TO PAGE 36.

You suffer the indignity of being hauled off to a tented area for servants. A smelly, filthy woman hands you a flimsy piece of fabric, which is supposed to be some kind of garment. "In there," she orders gruffly, pointing to a curtained corner in the tent. "Change, and be quick about it."

You shudder as you pull on the dress. What are they going to have you do? You step back out, and the woman looks at you disapprovingly. "Too soft," she says. "You'll never last."

That's what you're worried about. "I—I've heard that these are very dangerous men," you say. "That they . . . that the skeletons . . ." You're not sure how to phrase this. After all, this woman could be one of the rebellious slaves who slaughtered their masters!

The woman bursts out laughing, showing several missing teeth.

You gape at her.

TURN TO PAGE 96

You and Dastan arrive at the city of Avrat and join the end of the long funeral procession as it approaches the entrance. Two towering granite leopards stand sentry at the gates.

You eye the surroundings nervously. "There's got to be a hundred Persian soldiers watching those gates."

"Maybe more," Dastan agrees.

This is ridiculous. Dastan will get caught, and you will lose the Dagger forever. "Please!" you beg. "We must take the Dagger north. There's a Guardian Temple hidden in the mountains outside Alamut. Only the priests know of it. If the holy city is occupied, it's the only place the Dagger can rest safely."

He ignores you and keeps walking.

"Dastan, why do you think your father took you off the street that day?" you ask.

This gets his attention.

"Why would a king take a poor boy from the streets into his own family?"

"I suppose he felt something for me."

"Love?" you suggest. "He very well may have." You pause, trying to find the right words. "But that's not what was at work. It was something far greater—the gods have a plan for you. A destiny."

Dastan just laughs.

TURN TO PAGE 49

"Perhaps you're right," you say. "I could use some help." You don't tell the genie where you're going or what your mission is. You still don't trust him.

You lead Astrella outside and mount her. The rain has stopped and the sky is clearing. You turn back and see Kartosh hovering at the mouth of the cave. "Well, are you coming?"

"Invite me to join you," he says sternly.

You roll your eyes. Is he doing this to be irritating? If he wants to be catered to and flattered all the time, he's not going to be a very pleasant companion. "Fine. Please, will you come out of the stupid cave and join me?"

Kartosh grins broadly and steps outside. He takes several deep breaths.

You frown. "I don't know if Astrella can carry us both," you tell him. "I can't have you slowing me down. Maybe this isn't such a good idea."

You watch as he kneels down and starts digging in the mud in front of the cave. Great. Is he going to waste your time making mud pies?

Then you realize he's making a model of a horse. He stands and intones an incantation. You blink, and there, before you, is a living, breathing full-size horse!

"I have a ride of my own, thank you very much," Kartosh says. "Let's see who the slow one is now!"

He takes off at a gallop, leaving you standing there staring after him.

TURN TO PAGE 39

Dastan's voice hardens. "Don't make the mistake of thinking you know me, Princess."

Before you can figure out what he means, you arrive at the entrance to the great hall.

"Wait here with Her Highness," Dastan instructs the Persian soldier at the doorway. Then he turns to you. "If you can manage it, I suggest a hint of humility when you're presented to the king. For your own good."

He leaves you standing in the corridor with the guard. You listen to the festive party going on inside, angered by the partygoers' happiness.

Finally, the beefy guard beside you receives some kind of signal. He grips your arm and opens the doors to the great hall. It pains you to see these invaders celebrating in the same room where you have held banquets for your allies and visiting dignitaries; where as a small child you would play hide-and-seek with indulgent attendants. Now a different king sits on the dais, and men with weapons watch your every move.

TURN TO PAGE 105

"I was expecting golden statues and waterfalls," Amar complains. You just grin. You slowly and carefully make your way down the mountain.

Dastan takes the opportunity to walk beside you. "You're descended from her, aren't you?" he asks softly. "The girl that won man his reprieve."

You nod. "Her descendants are Guardians. Alamut's royal family, priests of this temple. We are trained from childhood to embody the virtue of our ancestor. So that, like her, we can stand before the gods as symbols of man's goodness."

Dastan shakes his head, disbelieving.

"It's a sacred obligation, Dastan," you say. "Passed down by blood through generations."

You enter the village and stop to look at him. "Your real parents. What do you know of them?"

"King Sharaman was my real parent," he replies. His face grows serious. "Before he died he asked me if I would be more than a good man. If I'd be a great man."

"He sensed your calling."

You can tell he's not so sure about this.

"It is not something you ask for, Dastan," you add.

Now he nods, as if he finally understands the responsibility of destiny. He pulls out the Dagger and holds it out to you. "Don't cut yourself, Princess," he says.

TURN TO PAGE 86

Nizam and Dastan greet the king as he dismounts. King Sharaman is delighted to see them both. "And who is this lovely creature?" he asks, smiling at you.

"This is Princess Tamina," Dastan says, rolling his eyes at the word *lovely*. "Tus requests that you bless his union with her. He believes it will create a strong alliance between our empires."

The king nods. "What say you, Princess?"

This is your final chance. "I will agree, but on one condition."

"Captive princesses don't make the terms," Nizam warns.

"Let her speak," the king says.

You give the man a grateful look. "Prince Dastan has in his possession a dagger. It is a sacred object to my people. I only ask that it be returned to me."

You see Sharaman considering, and it looks as if he's about to agree. But then Nizam speaks. "I have an idea. As a symbolic gesture, we keep the Dagger and give her one of our sacred relics. It will deepen our exchange."

"Marvelous idea," the king says, nodding approvingly.

Now Nizam faces you. "I'll just take the Dagger now."

Dastan gives you a quizzical look, then hands Nizam the Dagger.

A few days later, the world goes fuzzy. The next thing you know, you're a small child playing on the streets of Alamut. Your parents are talking about King Nizam, who rules the powerful Persian Empire.

You ignore them. It is the way it has always been . . . isn't it?

THE END

"Who are you?" you ask.

"Who's asking?" the being snaps.

"A very weary traveler, who simply sought shelter from the storm." You aren't going to reveal your true identity. "And I'm far too tired to play guessing games."

"I'm never tired of games!" the being says. "And I had so hoped we'd be friends."

"I don't make friends with those who won't identify themselves," you counter. "I've never seen anyone quite like you."

"That's because you haven't been looking," the being says. "My kind are everywhere." His voice takes on a hypnotic quality, as if reciting an incantation. "In the shimmer of heat in the desert. At the threshold. Waiting at the crossroads. We inhabit the in-between places."

You gape at him. What he is describing—that's what is said of the genie! They are mysterious creatures—perhaps angels, perhaps demons. No one is certain. They can bring great luck and good fortune, or create disaster and torment.

"My name is Kartosh," says the genie. "And now, by rights, you must tell me yours."

"Esmedina," you lie. You will need to tread carefully here. Genie are remarkably unpredictable.

TURN TO PAGE 76

"That whirling sand is meant for me?" you ask.

"It's how the cult of Hassansins travel," Kartosh explains. "And they are persistent. Not to mention deadly."

You knew that there would be those intent on stealing the Dagger to use for their own evil purposes. But Hassansins? You have heard of their deadly skill. If the Dagger of Time were to fall into their hands, it could mean the end of all humanity.

"You seem to know about my foe," you say. "How can I defeat them?"

"You can't," the genie says. "But I can."

He watches as the sand dervishes come closer. Then he faces you. "One of my many skills is shape-shifting," he tells you. "I can take your form and lead them on a merry chase. That would mean you'd continue on alone, though. And they may not fall for the ruse."

"Or?" you ask.

He shrugs. "We fight them, and if we win we won't have to worry about them anymore. But they are powerful warriors."

It's up to you. Both seem like very risky choices.

Do you stand and fight? TURN TO PAGE 110.

Or do you want Kartosh to pretend to be you?
TURN TO PAGE 128.

Joining the dignitaries seems to be your best bet. You use your charms on a servant master to get you and Dastan a job with one of the many royal visitors arriving for the funeral. You're assigned to a Mughal sultan. He is obese, with rolls of wobbling fat that wiggle as his porters lift his platform and carry him on their shoulders.

Dastan is one of those suffering, struggling porters. You walk beside him, carrying a silver nutcracker and a basket of walnuts. From time to time the sultan reaches down and you hand up some nuts.

"You couldn't find someone lighter?" Dastan gasps, straining.

You hide your smile. "The Mughals of the Hindu Kush are a noble people. You should be honored."

The sultan passes gas, and Dastan winces at the terrible stench. "Yes, I feel terribly honored."

The soldiers at the gate step forward for inspection. You hold your breath, hoping they won't recognize Dastan as he struggles with the others to hold the sultan aloft.

Luckily, the Sultan's digestive issues work in your favor. The soldiers quickly wave you through, their noses wrinkled in disgust.

TURN TO PAGE 109

If Prince Dastan was in the palace, your maidservant would have been gossiping about him. After all, he's a very handsome and powerful young man. So you're going to search for him *outside* the palace compound.

But first, you want to make a quick stop at the laundry. You follow the secret passageway to the servants' quarters. You know there's a well-hidden exit between the kitchen and the laundry. Perfect.

You slip out, and the disguised panel slides back into place. Good. No one saw you. You hurry to the laundry.

In the midday heat, there are almost no servants working. You understand why—with the massive vats of boiling water the temperature is almost unbearable. You rush through the washing room. You need to get to the drying area. You want a change of wardrobe.

You scan the room filled with clothes hanging out to dry and grab what you need. This morning you started as a princess, then you took your maidservant's attire. Now you're going off into the city—dressed as a young man.

TURN TO PAGE 117

You wake in a panic. There's a hand clamped over your mouth! You try to scream until you realize it's Dastan looming over you.

He points to a Persian patrol cresting a nearby dune, barely visible in the first rays of dawn. *Ah.* He didn't want you to alert them he was here. You make it clear you won't scream and he removes his hand. That's when you notice—the caravan is gone!

"Where did the tribesmen go?" you ask.

"Bedouins set out early," Dastan explains. "Especially if they're trying to ditch someone. Judging from your tracks, you were slowing them down. Or maybe it was your penchant for lies and backstabbing."

You scowl, but you have to admit he has a point. "I had no choice but to leave you." You study his careworn face. "I take it your uncle didn't listen to you."

"Worse than that," he says, settling beside you. "While we spoke, I saw his hands had been burned. He said it happened trying to pull free the poisoned cloak that killed my father." He shakes his head. "I turned it over in my mind a hundred times. My uncle made no move to touch that cloak."

"So the burns . . ." you say, piecing it together.

"He must have been the one who poisoned it. It wasn't Tus, it was Nizam."

"I'm sorry, Dastan." You know this is difficult for him. You can't imagine what it would be like to be betrayed in such terrible ways by the people you called your family.

 TURN TO PAGE 16

"**W**hat about the Dagger?" Dastan asks.

"Given to the girl whose goodness won man his reprieve," you answer. "It's meant to be used in defense of the Sandglass. The Dagger blade is the only thing that can pierce the glass and remove the Sands of Time."

Dastan nods, showing he understands. "But if one were to place the Dagger in the Sandglass and press the jewel button at the same time—"

"Sand would flow through endlessly." You finish for him.

"And you could turn back time as far as you like!"

"Yes," you admit. "But this is forbidden. History is a book written by the gods. Changing it is an abuse of their gift."

"My uncle saved my father's life when they were children," Dastan says, realization dawning on his face. "He means to go back in time and undo what he did. Let my father die! That would make Nizam king for a lifetime!"

You fear he is right. That his uncle's greed and ambition will make him use the Dagger in such a way—if he gets his hands on it. You have to make Dastan understand how catastrophic that would be.

 TURN TO PAGE 13

Your head whips back and forth searching for a way to create a diversion. Then you see it—the ostrich pen!

You sidle over to the pen and kick the latch free. The birds stampede onto the track, disrupting the race and angering the crowd. Amar's men pour onto the track trying to catch the squawking creatures. You see Dastan leap over the railing onto the track, dodging ostriches as he chases the Dagger. Amar's men start going after him.

You fling open a cage filled with weapons. "Hey! Over here!" you shout to the crowd. You toss weapons out, causing a full-fledged riot.

You run toward Dastan just as he knocks out the man with your dagger. "Get to the tunnel!" you cry.

You race through a tunnel leading to the valley. You hear a loud scraping sound and see a gate dropping down from the ceiling. You charge forward, drop, and roll under the gate. The gate hits the ground with a thud.

With Dastan on the other side.

"Pull the lever," he says, pointing to the wall. "It will open the gate!"

Amar and his men are closing in.

"Give me the Dagger," you say.

Dastan glances over his shoulder, then back at you. "This is not the time!" he shouts. "Now pull it!"

"Give me the Dagger!" you insist.

Suddenly, he pulls his sword and thrusts it at you through the bars!

 TURN TO PAGE 82

"Stop it!" you scold yourself, your voice echoing back to you. You are a Guardian, not a helpless maid. Astrella snorts and her ears twitch. You pat her neck. "Sorry, girl," you say. "Didn't mean to startle you."

Another crash of lightning makes her whinny. You cluck at her. "Okay, we'll go in even farther. Get you away from the cave's entrance."

You carefully bring the mare deeper into the cave. Not carefully enough. You trip over something and stumble onto the mucky ground.

You feel around to find out what tripped you. It's a satchel. Someone must have left it here. You open it and pull out two things: a large, highly decorated jar. Tracing its raised design with your fingers, you guess its covered in images of wild creatures and exotic plants. It feels heavy, so you know something's inside. The other thing is a tiny box that appears to be covered in gold leaf and precious gems. It feels empty.

Which should you open?

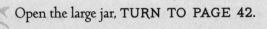

Open the large jar, TURN TO PAGE 42.

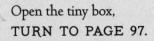

Open the tiny box,
TURN TO PAGE 97.

You leap onto the column, clutching it as it crashes down, creating a bridge between you and the Sandglass. The impact knocks Nizam over, and he drops the Dagger. You race after it, and more shaking throws you to the ground. You lie there stunned.

So close! Your fingers touch the Dagger's handle. *Yes!*

Nizam lunges at you, desperate for the Dagger. You tuck and roll out of his way, and he falls into the chasm, screaming the whole way down.

You roll onto your back and clutch the Dagger to your chest. You shut your eyes and breathe hard, trying to get up the strength to stand.

"Strange spot for a nap," you hear Dastan say.

You gaze up to see him standing over you, bloody and covered in dirt.

He holds out his hand and you take it.

It's over. The world is safe.

You smile at Prince Dastan. "We did it," you say, full of wonder. Then you smirk. "Let's get out of here. Someone could really use some cleaning up."

Prince Dastan feigns shock. "I hope you're not talking about *me*, Princess," he protests. "Have you seen a mirror?" Then he grows serious. "Before my father died, he made one last decree. Do you remember?"

You blush. You do. It was that you and the prince should marry. You find you are no longer horrified by the idea. In fact, you have a funny feeling that perhaps this, too, is part of your destiny.

THE END

You study Dastan's face, desperately hoping you've gotten through to him, and made him see the importance of your sacred duty. He gazes solemnly at the Dagger.

"The secret Guardian Temple outside Alamut is a sanctuary," you say. "The Dagger must be delivered back to the safety of this sacred home. It's the only way to stop this Armageddon. That's the truth, Dastan. Give me back the Dagger so I can take it there."

Dastan is clearly weighing his decision. Then, to your shock and horror, he slides the Dagger back into his belt.

"I'm sorry, Princess," he tells you. "I can't do that."

You stare at him, stunned.

Do you attack him to get the dagger back?
TURN TO PAGE 102.

Or do you try to find some other way to persuade him?
TURN TO PAGE 31.

At the word "dagger," Nizam's expression changes. "Why is your princess so concerned about a single dagger?"

Perhaps this was a mistake. He seems far too interested.

"I . . . I *think* it's a dagger," you say. You open your eyes wide, as if you aren't all that bright. "Maybe it was something else she wanted to get from Prince Dastan." You rack your brain trying to come up with a word a dim-witted servant might have mixed up with dagger. "Swagger? Yes, that's it! She wanted to know where he got his swagger!" Inwardly you groan. You can't believe *that* was all you could think of!

Nizam chuckles. "I wondered how you would talk yourself out of this one, but I had no idea it would be so funny. I never thought of princesses as being so . . . entertaining. Usually they are dull and spoiled."

You grow cold as you look at him.

"I know all about the Dagger, *Princess Tamina*," he says, his voice hardening. "Perhaps we can work together to wrest it out of Prince Dastan's hands."

This is a surprising twist. "There's one problem," you tell him. "I don't want you to have it any more than I want Prince Dastan to have it. So why should I help you?"

Nizam suddenly grips you by the throat. "If you do, I'll let you live. If you don't . . ." He squeezes harder.

"All right!" you gasp.

TURN TO PAGE 48

The genie's eyes narrow. He circles you.

"I know you're on a sacred quest," Kartosh says, surprising you. You had not told him that. "But what kind . . . I wonder. . . ."

You notice the rain has stopped. You should get away—quickly.

"Very nice to have met you," you say, taking Astrella's reins. "I really must be on my way."

In a flash, he blocks the mouth of the cave. "You released me from the box. I demand you take me with you."

"You *demand*?" you say.

"I could be very helpful." Kartosh wheedles. "I see danger around you. Perhaps I can afford you some protection."

Perhaps he could. Or perhaps *he's* the danger!

If you ask him to accompany you, TURN TO PAGE 61.

If you tell him he can't come with you,
TURN TO PAGE 54.

You don't think you'll be able to make the long journey on your own. You shout and wave to the Bedouin caravan, and they stop long enough for you to catch up.

You don't speak their language, but you manage to make yourself understood. Someone brings you a goatskin of water, another some dates and nuts. But it's clear they want to keep moving. A young boy leads a camel to you. You're going to have to ride the thing!

The boy gets the camel to kneel, and after several attempts to mount it, someone helps you climb aboard. Then the boy gives a signal, and the camel makes its jerky rise.

Whoa! It's hard to stay on as the camel starts walking. Even harder to control it. It definitely has a mind of its own.

"Hey!" you call. "Wait up!" The camel has decided it wants to go in a different direction. By the time you get it turned around, the rest of the group has traveled far ahead. You watch as they stop. The young boy rides back and grabs the camel's reins. You are terribly embarrassed, but that's the way you ride until they decide to stop for the night. Wandering a crooked path until the boy rescues you—again and again.

In the darkness, you lie on the ground, wrapped in one of the Bedouin's cloaks. Every single muscle aches. You quickly fall asleep.

TURN TO PAGE 69

It's just in time. Out of the sand funnels come powerful horses carrying black-clad fighters. The mud soldiers charge toward them. Astonishing! The battle is over in just minutes. The mud soldiers win!

Kartosh says another incantation and the mud soldiers melt away back into the ground.

"I-I don't know how to thank you," you tell Kartosh.

"A gift is customary," Kartosh snaps.

You laugh. "I'd hate to break with custom. So what would you like?"

He casts his eyes down. "What I'd really like . . . though I'll regret giving up the gold I usually demand . . . well . . ." He brings his eyes up to meet yours. "I'd like to continue on with you—even though we've defeated your enemies. I've been locked up in a box for a thousand years."

"Poor Kartosh," you say. "You must be so lonely."

He pretends to look insulted. "Me? Wanting the companionship of a mere human? I'd never be *that* lonely! I simply need instruction on the current times. So I'll fit in."

"I see," you say. His pleading expression makes it clear that he's simply too proud to admit his loneliness. "Well, I'd be happy to help you make the adjustment."

Relief floods his golden features. "You won't regret it!" He hops up onto his horse. "Well, quit dawdling. That dagger won't deliver itself!"

You grin, then realize you *never* mentioned the Dagger. You hope you won't regret this decision in . . .

THE END.

Your head feels a little fuzzy as you grab the sword from the saddle on Dastan's horse. Suddenly the prince is right there, gripping your wrist!

"Go for that sword again and I swear I'll break your arm," he hisses.

"Again?" you repeat. What does he mean? Then it hits you. Your eyes grow wide as you stare at the Dagger. It is just as you feared. Dastan has seen what the Dagger can do. Worse—"You used up all the sand!"

Dastan glances at the empty glass handle. He hits the jewel button. Nothing happens. "What *is* this?" he demands.

You pull hard, but he shakes you off. He's too amazed by the Dagger to pay you much mind.

"Incredible," he says, piecing it together. "Releasing the sand *turns back time!* And only the holder of the Dagger is aware of what's happened. He can go back, alter events, change time . . . and no one knows but him!" Now he looks right at you. "How much can it unwind?"

You can't believe he made the discovery! This is awful!

"Answer me, Princess!" he demands.

"You destroyed my city!" you scream at him.

"We had intelligence you were arming our enemies."

"You had the lies of a Persian spy," you say bitterly.

"Our invasion wasn't about weapons forges," he says. "It was about this dagger!"

"Clever prince," you mutter miserably.

 TURN TO PAGE 35

You look up at Dastan's face, wondering why he has pulled you aside.

He yanks the amulet you wear from around your neck. He turns so that Sheikh Amar and his men can't see him flip it open. He grins when he sees the glowing sand inside.

"Dastan, listen to me," you plead.

He ignores you and pours the sand into the glass handle of the Dagger. He slides the knife back into his belt, then hands you the empty amulet.

"When my uncle sees the power of the Dagger, he'll believe our invasion was a lie," he says. "Thank you, Your Highness."

You're desperate now. "Dastan, I know I haven't been completely honest with you—"

"But your lies have been so charming," he says sarcastically.

"That dagger is sacred. It's only allowed to leave Alamut if the city falls. It was being smuggled to safety when you stole it. Dastan, if the Dagger falls into the wrong hands—"

"Don't worry, Your Highness. I'll keep your knife safe."

"You don't understand what's at stake! *This is a matter for the gods, not man!*"

"*Your* gods, not mine." Dastan is clearly finished with this conversation. He turns and nods to one of Amar's men, who drags you away.

 TURN TO PAGE 59

You are escorted from the High Temple to your chambers. You are told to wait to be presented to the king and have your union with Prince Tus blessed. You are a prisoner in your own palace.

You do learn something important from the guard just before he plants himself outside your room: the handsome young man who now has your dagger is Prince Dastan, the youngest of the three princes. Garsiv is the name of the Persian who was harsh with you. Tus, as you've unfortunately learned, will inherit the crown. The man with the bald head is their uncle, Nizam.

You pace your chamber. You have to get the Dagger—it is not just your own life that hangs in the balance but the future of all of humanity. No one can discover its power. But how do you prevent that from happening?

What is the smartest thing to do? Should you find a way to search for Prince Dastan? Or should you try to find out more by allowing yourself to be presented to the king?

Sneak away ON PAGE 26.

Meet the king
ON PAGE 17.

You hold very still, terrified you've been gutted.

"Move, Princess," Dastan orders.

You slowly step to the side. Now you see that the blade has not impaled *you*, but one of Sheikh Amar's guards. He was standing right behind you, gripping a scimitar. He flops over.

You gape at Dastan. He just saved your life!

Dastan drops down and yanks the keys from the skewered guard's belt. He quickly fits a key into a lock and raises the gate. He spins and lowers it again just before Amar and his men reach you.

You race away, leaving the sheikh muttering and cursing after you.

It seems you are once again stuck traveling with Dastan to the city of Avrat. He has the Dagger, and until he doesn't you can't leave his side.

TURN TO PAGE 60

You shouldn't waste time investigating caves, you remind yourself. You have a mission to complete. And it has nothing to do with whoever—or whatever—tiled the tunnel floor.

You turn Astrella around. As you do, you hear a rumbling behind you.

"Who dares enter our sanctuary!" a voice booms. "Trespassing is punishable by death!" Thunderous footsteps shake the ground.

You quickly mount Astrella, your hands shaking. It's awkward in the narrow tunnel, especially while holding on to the torch, but you don't want her to try to run in the dark. As soon as you're settled on the saddle, you urge her to hurry. There is no way you want to see the body that goes with that voice.

You don't have to bother. Astrella navigates at top speed. Soon the footsteps recede and no one shouts after you anymore. You charge out of the cave. It's still raining but you don't care. You'd rather be out in the storm than trapped in the tunnel with whatever giant you offended!

You head north, vowing that you will take no more side trips! And you keep that promise all the way to your journey's . . .

END.

Amar's men set up camp in the oasis. Two guards stand watch, and everyone else rests around the campfire. Somehow you manage to fall asleep.

You wake abruptly to see Dastan, no longer bound. He is using the Dagger and a smoldering log to kill a group of vicious pit vipers!

Amar and Seso stare at him. "Persian, how did you do that?" Amar asks in a shaking voice.

"Seso saw reason and gave me the Dagger," Dastan explains. "The rest was just instinct." He slides the Dagger into his belt and winks at you.

You know exactly what happened. It had nothing to do with instinct. Dastan must have somehow been alerted to the presence of the vipers. He used the Dagger to rewind time. When time moved forward he knew the position of each of the deadly snakes and was ready for them.

"We have to get out of here, now," Dastan orders. He bends down and cuts the ropes binding you. "Hurry!"

His urgency is clear—Amar and Seso signal the men without an argument. Quickly, you mount horses and thunder away.

TURN TO PAGE 52

You can't risk the life of another to protect the Dagger. It is *your* destiny, *your* responsibility. You will take the journey north to the Guardian Temple as you have been instructed to do. This is the only place it will be safe.

You remember all the stories you've been told, the directions you were required to learn. There is no map—for security reasons the location of the temple has never been written down. It is passed on from one generation of Guardians to the next.

Quickly donning a disguise, you sneak to one of the stables and mount your horse, Astrella. After several well-placed, generous bribes, you ride out of the city, wary of the Persian army.

You know there will be certain landmarks to guide you, along with the stars. You hope you remember all the twists and turns. A flutter of anxiety rises in your chest.

You have trained for this moment all your life, you remind yourself. Failure is not an option.

 TURN TO PAGE 40

You take the Dagger from Dastan and smile. You turn and survey the village.

"It's quiet," he comments.

You nod, your heart starting to thump in your chest. Something feels wrong. You notice a farmhouse door is ajar. It's a cold day. Why would they . . . ?

Anxiety mounting, you run to the farmhouse and rush inside, Dastan is right behind you. "There's nobody here," he says.

You hear Seso reciting some kind of prayer out back. You and Dastan duck back outside. You gasp.

Four dead bodies are slumped against the house, their throats slit. They were Guardians.

You drop to your knees beside the bodies.

"They have been dead a long time," Seso says. "Tortured first."

"These wounds aren't from normal weapons," Dastan says ominously.

"Hassansins?" Seso asks.

"They were here. Nizam knows!" Dastan exclaims.

Then Amar approaches with a more terrible announcement. "All dead. The entire village."

TURN TO PAGE 33

You decide to be blunt. "Prince, there's something you must know," you say. "Your uncle, he's not who you think he is."

Dastan raises an eyebrow. "Oh, really?"

You have to tread carefully—you don't want to offend him. You need his help. "Just take care," you say. "I don't know that you can trust him."

Dastan laughs. "You don't know my uncle."

"Perhaps it is *you* who doesn't know your uncle," you say, temper flaring. "I believe he poses a great danger."

Dastan's eyes grow cold. "To you, perhaps. After all, your people have been arming our enemies. You are the one who should take care, Princess."

You have to press on. Clearly, warning him about his uncle is only making things worse. Perhaps you should take a different approach.

"I came to find you because you have something that means a great deal to me," you say. "And I would like it back."

TURN TO PAGE 28

Prince Dastan grips your arm and pulls you up the steps leading to the gates of the city. "Behave yourself, or you will suffer the consequences."

"I am already suffering," you spit at him. "And you have no idea what consequences there will be if you don't listen to me!"

He turns to one of the musicians assembled to greet the king. "Can you start playing now?" he asks. "I want to drown out this annoying buzz." He tips his head, indicating he means *you*.

"I will not stop until I get the Dagger," you warn him.

"Princess, I was happy to take your advice at sport," he says, clearly out of patience. "But it would be unwise for you to try to tell me what to do. How stupid do you think I must be to take orders from an enemy?"

You stare at him in disbelief. He doesn't know who the true enemy is.

"Your uncle Nizam—" you begin.

"Is right here." Nizam steps up beside you. "How nice of you to greet the king with us, Princess Tamina."

You glare at him even as your heart sinks. They will never believe that Nizam poses a threat. You've exhausted all your options. Now you're going to have to find some way to convince the *king* to give you the Dagger.

TURN TO PAGE 64

It is up to you to lead the way. You're the only one who knows the location of the Guardian Temple.

You bring the group high up into the mountains, making your way along dizzying switchbacks and zigzagging up a perilous cliff face. You emerge from clouds of heavy mist into a forest. You scan the area and find the nearly invisible trail.

"Excuse the humble confusion of a former salt slave," Sheikh Amar says, shivering with cold, "but how the devil do you know where you're going?"

"I memorized this path as a child," you explain. "Every princess must. It is sacred."

Amar rolls his eyes, but he and Seso continue on.

Dastan pauses and looks at you, clearly wanting the rest of the story. You think if you tell him more, perhaps they'll be reassured of their mission.

"After the girl won man's reprieve from the gods, she was told to travel by faith to a place of divine beauty. There she found the stone which held an emblem of the gods' trust in her. The Dagger of Time."

Finally, you are able to peer through the mist down to the valley below. Nestled among the trees are a few simple stone houses.

"We've made it," you announce. You can finish the story later.

TURN TO PAGE 63

"In Alamut rests the breathing heart of all life on earth," you say. "The Sandglass of the Gods."

The wind continues to howl outside. Dastan gazes at you, transfixed.

"Long ago, the gods looked down at man and saw nothing but greed and treachery. And so they sent a great sandstorm to destroy all, wipe clean the face of the earth."

You shiver, despite the heat. A sandstorm not unlike the one raging around us, you think.

"Go on." Dastan encourages you.

"But one young girl survived. She begged the gods to give mankind another chance, offering her life in exchange. The gods looked down on her, and seeing the purity within, were reminded of man's potential for good. So they returned man to earth and swept the sands into the Sandglass."

Aksh whinnies, nervous in the storm. You and Dastan both pat him reassuringly.

"The glass embodies our existence," you explain. "As long as the sand runs through it, time moves forward and man's survival is assured. The Sandglass controls time itself. Reminds us our lives are in the gods' hands. That we are mortal."

TURN TO PAGE 70

The caves look foreboding, so you head through the gates. You may be able to find supplies, help, and safe cover to wait out the storm.

Astrella snorts nervously as you trot into the center of what seems to be a completely abandoned city. What happened here? you wonder. Why did everyone leave?

"Hello?" you call. You peer down side streets and into windows. Astrella's hooves make loud clip-clopping sounds that echo around you, adding to the spooky atmosphere. You notice in some of the homes there are places set at tables, as if the inhabitants were about to sit down to dinner. Shops are open for business without shopkeepers. It's an eerie place.

A loud clap of thunder startles you and Astrella. She rears up, neighing frantically, and you nearly lose your balance. "It's all right," you murmur, patting her neck as she settles back to the ground. "We'll just wait out the storm, then leave at once."

Lightning crackles across the sky and suddenly you're drenched by a torrential downpour. "Let's go!" you shout, kicking the mare with your heels. You guide Astrella into what had been a bustling bazaar. Now the canopies cover unattended goods, and there aren't any customers.

You dismount and tie Astrella to a post. The rain pummels the fabric above you, but it seems as if it's going to hold.

You wander the bazaar, trying to understand why the shopkeepers abandoned their stalls.

 TURN TO PAGE 11

The crowd parts to let you through. Everyone is wondering who would be so bold.

Dastan smirks. "You're saying you can do the wall run?"

"You're saying I can't?" you say, keeping your voice low. "Want to make a wager?"

He looks at you, and you're worried he may be on to you. And that you won't actually be able to do it. But it seems like the best way to get the Dagger back. Perhaps, even if you fail, attempting this stunt will move you into his inner circle and afford you another opportunity at the Dagger.

"Sure, I'll make a bet," Dastan says. "Didn't you just hear me say I'd give a prize to anyone who can do it?"

You nod. "Then let's stop talking and start running," you say.

Dastan grins and gestures to Roham, who is still standing at the wall. "Be my guest."

You face Roham, and you're about to run toward him when you decide you'd better take off your shoes. They're much too big for you—they'll only slow you down.

You notice Dastan looking quizzically at your feet, but you can't let him rattle you. This is for the Dagger.

 TURN TO PAGE 115

The decision has been made. "I will tell you everything," you promise. "But please, can we get out of here first?"

Dastan smirks. "Only a princess would think she can outrun a sandstorm." You watch nervously as Dastan pulls Aksh to the ground, and using the saddle blanket and sword, creates a tent against the horse. He gestures formally. "Your Highness."

You sit under the blanket and Dastan drops down beside you. The storm wails around you.

For a while, the only sound is your breathing and the howling winds outside. Finally, Dastan breaks the silence. "I know Nizam needs the Dagger, that he's got our army searching Alamut for more of the sand, but what else?" he says. "What secret lies under your city?"

This is the moment of truth. You hope you have put your faith in the right man. What you are about to tell him no one but the Guardians know. You take a deep breath and begin.

 TURN TO PAGE 90

You turn back to the woman. "This place makes you younger? That's amazing!"

"No, no," Chazika murmurs. "It doesn't work like that. We stay the age we were when we arrived. I don't know why your horse . . ."

A scream behind her startles you both. You look beyond her and see that something terribly wrong is happening to the people by the pool.

Your eyes widen in horror. They're turning into bizarre half-old/half-young beings. A man's head sits atop a toddler's body. A beautiful woman is young and blond on one side of her face and head and wrinkled and gray on the other!

"You—there's something shimmering around you," Chazika whispers as if she's in terrible pain. "An energy field of some sort. You are doing this to us!"

"I'm sorry! I don't know why . . . how . . ." Then it hits you. The Dagger of Time. It must be causing these strange transformations. After all, this place already is a time anomaly. The Dagger also affects time. The two forces together must be producing this effect.

"You must go," Chazika gasps. "Quickly!"

TURN TO PAGE 127

You think it best to start in the palace. You know your way around, and Prince Dastan is likely to be involved with preparing for the king's arrival. Your teeth clench as you realize he's also probably engaged in the excavations to search for weapons forges that the Persians are convinced are here, but you *know* are not.

You continue along the secret passage, making sure to count your steps. You don't want to accidentally come out of the door into the chambers being used by your husband-to-be, Tus, the next king of Persia.

You arrive at the doorway you want—it opens into the plaza in the center of the compound. So many times in the past you and your maids have enjoyed a cool breeze or admired the stars without even leaving the palace. But things are different now. You're not going to lounge on one of the relaxing chaises. The plaza is where you hope to pick up the scent of your dagger's whereabouts.

Behind the door you listen, your heart pounding. You hope no one will notice when you suddenly appear out of the wall. You touch the special code, and the door slides open. Designed to look like a fresco, the secret door is conveniently positioned out of the sight of visitors to the plaza. A large plant stands in front of it.

You slip out and quickly touch the corresponding code to close the door. In a flash, the door simply looks like a painted wall again.

Now to track down Prince Dastan—and your dagger.

TURN TO PAGE 46

The woman hoots even louder and then wipes tears of laughter from her eyes with a stained rag. "That Sheikh Amar," she says, "he was right! Put up those skeletons, spread a few rumors, and people will believe the worst. Which is just what he wants."

You're completely confused. "I don't understand."

"The big boss, Sheikh Amar," she explains, handing you a tray, "he came up with the idea when the mine owner died. Tell everyone that there was a terrible uprising and that the workers were vicious murderers. All to keep out the tax collectors!"

You stare at her. This is unbelievable.

"Of course," the woman concedes, loading up your tray with fermented goat milk, "many of them are powerful warriors. Like Seso, the large African man. I wouldn't want him angry at me."

You nod, remembering the muscular man with the shaved head.

"And watch out," she adds. "Ancient tribal feuds can flare up out of nowhere!"

"I'll remember," you say sincerely. This woman may be rough around the edges, but she has given you valuable advice.

"Now, hurry on out there. The men will be wanting their drinks! This crazy sport seems to make them rowdy. And thirsty!"

With a shove, she pushes you out the other side of the tent. You're surprised to see a racetrack carved out of the abandoned salt mine. And even more surprised to see what's racing—ostriches!

TURN TO PAGE 44

You hope the smaller box holds matches. You notice writing across the latch, but in the dim light it's hard to see. You're fairly certain it's in a language you don't know. You manage to get the complicated latch open—and a strange blue mist rises out of the box.

You don't believe it! A being of some sort is materializing!

You stare at the figure taking shape before your very eyes. He is large, with an elaborate headdress. His long nose is pierced, and he wears multiple rings in his ears. In fact, he seems to be dripping in jewels—necklaces, rings, bracelets. His skin is a strange, glittering gold, as if he's encased in the precious metal. He points at you and that's when you notice—he has too many fingers on each hand!

"Why have you disturbed my rest?" the being demands.

"I didn't mean to," you say. You hold the box out to him. "Here. You can go back in."

The being stretches his body. He's gigantic now.

"Do I look like I'd fit in that box?" he booms.

"Well, no, but you fit into it before," you point out.

"Oh, you'd like that, wouldn't you," he demands in an accusing voice. He suddenly shrinks down small enough to fit into the palm of your hand. "To lock me away. To make me so small you could crush me. Well, that's not going to happen!" He expands again with a whoosh. Now he's the size of a large man.

What is going on? Who—or what—*is* this strange being?

 TURN TO PAGE 65

You stare at the handsome young prince. Could it be true? Did he actually try to kill his own father? What kind of man is he?

The king sinks to the ground. "Dastan," he chokes out, "why?"

Dastan races up onto the dais and kneels beside his father. He cradles the king's head. "Father!" he cries.

But it's clear, the king is already dead.

"Seize him!" Garsiv shouts. "Seize the murderer!"

Chaos erupts around you as Prince Dastan tries to make his escape. This is a completely unforeseen situation. Everyone seems to have forgotten you. What should you do? You can't just run away—that wouldn't get you back the Dagger.

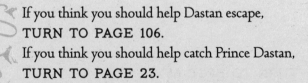

If you think you should help Dastan escape,
TURN TO PAGE 106.

If you think you should help catch Prince Dastan,
TURN TO PAGE 23.

Astrella thunders out of the city at a fast gallop. You want to put as many miles as possible between you and the ghosts. You don't even mind getting drenched by the rain.

"Use the Dagger!" you hear. You feel the strange tugging sensation again.

Oh, no! They've followed you out of the city!

"I thought—but you can't—" you sputter. "Don't you have to stay in the city? Isn't the city what you're haunting?"

The ghosts fly along beside you. "We only waited there for you to come. We will never leave you until you use the Dagger!"

"Fine!" You yank Astrella to a stop. "I'll use it. Then maybe you'll see that it won't work."

You press the jewel on the Dagger handle. The Sands of Time trickle out, glittering in the air around you. This is the Dagger's true power—why ghosts and men alike want it. Time rewinds. You're back up on Astrella telling the ghosts you'll use the Dagger.

"You see?" you declare. "It won't help you. The Dagger only holds enough sand to go back in time one minute!"

"No!" the ghosts wail. "You lie! You will never be rid of us until you take us back in time!"

You realize in horror that they mean this threat, that you can't escape them. They will whisper and wheedle and tug at you for the rest of time. You will slowly go mad in . . .

THE END.

Your curiosity overcomes you. You have to find out the mystery of the tiles. Who uses the same symbols as the Guardians?

The tiles continue on the ground, and soon the walls, too, are covered in decorative mosaics. You no longer have any sense of being in a cave, inside a mountain. You feel as if you're walking though a corridor in the High Temple. Astrella has calmed completely; she must also be feeling the same sense of familiarity.

The corridor opens into a large chamber, with vaulted ceilings, incense braziers, several low chaises, and scattered tables. Sitting on one of the chaises is a young girl. She's smiling.

You stare at her. She has the same henna tattoos that cover your own body, and she wears the same amulet you wear around your neck.

You know that face! This is the girl who saved humankind by begging the gods for mercy. Her pure spirit protected the world many long years ago. She is the original Guardian of the Dagger of Time.

She is . . . your ancestor.

 TURN TO PAGE 129

Accompanied by a lone guard, you hurry to the gates that lead out of the city. Your mind is reeling. Just get the Dagger, you tell yourself. Worry about everything else once that's accomplished.

You hear men cheering and shouting. It seems like a good place to start. You follow the sound around the corner and find a group of soldiers crowded together. They're placing bets as two men face each other. Each wields a massive barrel-shaped club. They clobber each other. The smaller fighter is taking the brunt of the blows, but he's holding his own. As he spins and lashes out, you recognize him.

It's Prince Dastan.

TURN TO PAGE 25

How dare he! You let out a shriek and fling yourself at Dastan, but he easily overpowers you.

"You know, I *was* going to help you," he says through gritted teeth. "But I'm sick and tired of your constant attacks!"

He shoves you away.

Your heart sinks. You were so close to retrieving the Dagger! What can you do?

"Please . . ." you begin.

Dastan holds up a hand to stop you. "Not another word. If you say one more thing, not only will I take the Dagger away, I'll leave you here alone in the desert."

That shuts you up. Then you come up with a great idea.

You throw yourself at him again and grab at the Dagger in his belt. But you don't try to yank it away—you just press the jewel in the handle. All you want to do is release a few grains of sand.

Just enough to go back in time—and *not* attack him!

GO BACK TO PAGE 74 and make a different choice!

You see Nizam enter. You feel Dastan stiffen beside you. He steps out of the shadows. You watch as the two men face each other in the glowing light of the Sandglass, swords drawn.

You have to do something. But what?

"You murdered your own family!" Dastan cries. "King Sharaman was your brother!"

"And my curse!" Nizam snaps back.

The ground rumbles as another earthquake hits. You steady yourself against the column and watch in fear as pieces of the ceiling cave in. Nizam lashes at Dastan with the Dagger, slashing him across the gut. To your horror there's another quake—and this time the floor breaks away!

You scream as Dastan drops into a crevasse, his arms and legs windmilling wildly. He grabs a jagged rock and stops his fall.

Nizam clutches the massive structure that holds the Sandglass. He begins to crawl up the platform.

"Go no further!" you shout at him. You have to stop him. But how? There's an enormous chasm between you and the Sandglass.

There is another cataclysmic quake, and the column beside you starts to topple.

TURN TO PAGE 73

How could I have let him get away with the Dagger? you think, berating yourself. You scan the area, then spot him dashing across the rooftops. Is he insane?

You rush after the procession, banging into people, slipping in and out of the crowd. You've lost sight of Dastan, but you have no doubt where he is headed—to his uncle at the front of the royal retinue.

You frantically dodge horse hooves and guards, desperate now. What if Dastan gets caught? Who will take possession of the Dagger then?

Beads of sweat trickle down your back as you ignore the crush of mourners and continue to run. A cloaked man keeps step beside you. You try to lose him, but the street is too narrow here.

"Difficult but not impossible," the man says.

You glance up—into Dastan's face! You scowl. "Or more proof that you're insane!"

He grins, and you know that he got his message through.

Well, if nothing else, Prince Dastan is certainly resourceful!

 TURN TO PAGE 114

As you enter the grand room, you see that Prince Dastan is giving the king a gift. You watch as the king lifts up a prayer robe— the prayer robe of your own regent! The king smiles and puts it on as, silently, you seethe.

"What can I give you in return?" the king asks Prince Dastan.

Dastan gestures to you. "This is Princess Tamina," he says. "My brother Tus wishes to make a union with her people through marriage. It's my deepest wish that this win your approval."

The king studies you a moment, then stands and bows his head. "In all my travels I've never laid eyes on a more beautiful city, Your Highness."

"You should have seen it before your horde of camel-riding illiterates descended upon it," you reply. Then you add, shooting Dastan a glare, "But thank you for noticing, Your Highness."

TURN TO PAGE 24

Where the Dagger goes, you go. So that means you must help Dastan. You see a guard sneaking up behind the prince, sword drawn. Grabbing the nearest heavy object—a brass vase—you charge into the fray.

Thunk! You slam the vase into the guard's head, and he drops to the ground. As the man falls, you whirl and fling the vase into the face of another guard.

Dastan stares at you, stunned, then grabs you by the waist. He yanks you clear as a sword whistles by. It misses you by just a few inches. Then he drags you onto the balcony. You let out a shriek as he pulls you up and over the banister!

Splash! You land in the fountain in the courtyard below.

You scramble back up to your feet, hair streaming, clothes heavy with water.

"What do you think you're doing?" Dastan sputters.

"You may occupy this city," you tell him, "but you don't know its secrets. I can get us out of here!"

Not waiting for an answer, you head to the stables to find a ride, Dastan close behind.

TURN TO PAGE 34

"You'll never even make it to Avrat," you call after him. "Your plan is suicide!"

Dastan stops the horse and turns to look at you, his eyes burning. "My brother murdered my father and framed me for the crime. If I die trying to set that right, so be it." He faces forward and Aksh starts walking again.

"You're going to leave me here? In the middle of nowhere?" you shout. How can he ignore you this way? After you helped him escape, he's just going to abandon you?

Begging isn't working. You try another tack. "Noble Dastan," you say, your voice dripping with disdain and sarcasm, "abandoning a helpless woman in the wilderness? What does your precious honor say about that?"

You must have gotten to him. The horse comes to a stop.

You run to catch up. As much as you hate it, you have to accompany him as he tries to clear his name. You have to go where the Dagger goes, even if it's into the dreaded Valley of the Slaves. At least, until you come up with some other plan.

TURN TO PAGE 55

You decide the best way to stay dry is by getting to higher ground. Astrella resists a bit, but you take the tunnel that has a pathway leading sharply up.

The slope is steep, but the ground isn't muddy at all. In fact, you realize, thanks to the light shed by the torch, soon the dirt gives way to . . . tiles?

Bewildered, you continue on. Could someone live here?

You grow apprehensive. Maybe you should turn around. Yet you're so curious. And the tile—something about it looks familiar. The colors and patterns remind you of the decorative mosaics in the High Temple of Alamut. Could this be another Guardian outpost?

You've never heard of one, though. And Astrella is definitely nervous.

What should you do?

 If you want to keep going, TURN TO PAGE 100.

If you think this is far too strange and you want to turn around, TURN TO PAGE 83.

Inside the city, crowds line the streets, letting out a mournful wail as the ornate wagon carrying the king's body passes. You keep your eye on Dastan as he watches the royal contingent. You recognize the bald man, Nizam, as his uncle. But you don't see his brothers.

Dastan seems concerned by their absence as well. "He's not coming," he says. "Tus is still in Alamut." He whirls to face you. "The sand that fuels the Dagger. There's more of it hidden there!"

He studies your face. You sigh and nod. There's no point in pretending.

"That's why Tus stays there. That's what our army is searching for!" He turns to watch the procession again. "I have to send my uncle a message to meet me."

You point out the bodyguards surrounding his uncle. "That's impossible!"

But it's too late—Dastan's gone!

TURN TO PAGE 104

"Let's stand and fight," you decide. "I don't want to keep looking over my shoulder, wondering when they'll be back."

"You do realize there are only two of us, and many of them," Kartosh says.

"I will understand if you want to run," you say. "I won't make you fight my battles."

Kartosh makes a tut-tut sound. "Stop playing it so tough, girl. I told you I'd help, and I stick to my word." He dismounts and begins digging in the dirt. You give him a confused look. "I said I'd *help*!" he scolds. "I didn't say I'd take care of this single-handedly."

You climb down from Astrella. "What are we doing?" you ask, dropping down beside him.

"Making an army," he says. That's when you realize he's molding the dirt into soldiers! Just as he did with his horse, he's bringing these mud beings into life!

He says an incantation, and suddenly you are surrounded by dozens of fierce warriors.

TURN TO PAGE 78

"We're in this together," Dastan says.

You nod. You can't argue with him anymore—it will waste time. "Follow exactly in my footsteps," you instruct him. "Exactly!"

"I heard you the first time," Dastan snaps.

"Nothing can touch the surface other than where I step." You hope he understands how serious this is.

He nods and you begin the careful walk across the chamber, first this way, then that. All around you the rumbling continues. You fear the entire structure will collapse before you can get to the Sandglass!

You make it safely to the cupola and race down the winding stairs leading deep underground. You dodge falling debris as you run through the final tunnel. You hear Dastan following right behind you. You stop suddenly and signal him to stay back. You both duck behind a column and peer out.

Towering over the massive chamber is the gigantic Sandglass.

TURN TO PAGE 103

112

You can't abandon Dastan. You turn to face the Hassansins, gripping the Dagger.

The Persian army, which just a moment ago had their weapons trained on you, now start fighting the Hassansins. Dastan fights beside his brother; Seso and Amar bravely face the enemy with whatever they can get their hands on to use as weapons.

But it seems the pit vipers are trained to seek out the Dagger. They ignore your friends and head straight to you. Very quickly they surround you.

You slash at them, but it's no use. There are too many of them. The moment you kill one, another bites you. Then another. With weakening strength you watch first Garsiv, then Seso and Amar, and finally Prince Dastan, all succumb. Even the Persian guards with their crossbows can't outfight the vicious Hassansins.

You can't fight anymore either; the poison is rushing through your veins. Your knees buckle, and you collapse to the ground. The last thing you remember, before your eyes shut forever, is someone prying the Dagger from your fingers.

"I'm sorry," you whisper to the gods, your ancestor, and perhaps most of all, to Prince Dastan.

THE END

When you come to, you're alone and the Dagger is gone. You wonder how long you've been out.

You slowly find your way out of the cave, not knowing what you'll discover. Not knowing what to do next. You see that a terrible slaughter took place outside. The Hassansins are gone.

You find Dastan, kneeling beside his dead brother Garsiv.

"I'm sorry," you tell him.

"At the end, he believed me," Dastan says, his eyes full of pain. "Saved me, even."

You nod.

Now he looks at you more closely. "The Dagger?"

"It's gone," you confess. You feel so defeated, so . . . lost. "Protect the Dagger. No matter the consequences. That was my sacred duty. That was to be my destiny."

You look away, unable to meet his gaze. You don't want him to see the confusion and hopelessness in your eyes.

"We make our own destiny, Princess," Dastan declares. He takes your face in his hands and turns it. He looks deeply into your eyes. "We'll get it back," he promises.

TURN TO PAGE 15

Later that day, you accompany Dastan to the stables at the edge of the bazaar. This is where he is to meet with his uncle. His plan is to prove his innocence, but you have a plan of your own.

Dastan studies the crowd, and you realize he's spotted his uncle. The hooded man picks up a pomegranate. Dastan sidles up to him.

"You used to buy those for me when I was a boy," Dastan says.

"You would spit the seeds at Garsiv," the man replies, lowering his hood. Yes, it's Nizam. "You should not have asked me here, Dastan."

"I had no choice, Uncle."

Dastan grips his uncle's arm and nods at you. You nod back. Then he pulls Nizam into an empty livestock room. You stand where he can see you, acting as bodyguard.

For a few moments, anyway, you watch, but once they seem to be engaged in deep conversation you slip away. With the Dagger.

I wonder how Dastan will react when he discovers I replaced the Dagger with the sultan's silver nutcracker, you think. For a moment you feel a pang of regret—then shake it off.

You have to get the Dagger to safety. Let Dastan fend for himself.

TURN TO PAGE 58

You take a deep breath, focus, and race at the wall. You leap up and press off the wall with one foot, sending all your energy upward. You graze the wall with your other foot, twist in midair above Roham's head, and plant your foot again. The momentum brings you over him, and you push off again—this time somersaulting back to the ground. Amazingly, you land on your feet.

You did it!

Dastan gapes at you, but he's clapping as hard as everyone else. "Maybe I should take lessons from you," he says.

"Now for the promise," you remind him. "You said you'd give the man anything he wants."

"I said I'd give it to the *man*," Dastan says, stepping closer to you. He brings his lip to your ear and whispers, "not to the *princess*." He looks down at your bare feet and ankles. "Interesting tattoos."

Fear races through you like cold water. He *knows*.

You step away from him. "The prince is going back on his promise?" you demand. "I had no idea he had no honor."

Now the crowd begins to taunt Dastan, though they seem pretty good-natured. They're his men, after all.

But Dastan holds up a hand to quiet them. "I would never go back on a wager. Tell me, *sir*," he says, his eyes twinkling with amusement, "what is it you would like?"

 TURN TO PAGE 119

You force yourself not to smirk as Dastan reluctantly hands you the Dagger.

"Good luck with such a deceitful wretch as your bride," Dastan says to Tus as he stomps out of the room.

"Thank you," you say to Tus, slipping the Dagger into the waistband of your skirt. "It is nice to know that there are honorable Persians."

Tus smiles and gives you a little nod. "I hope this will set things straight with your maidservant's family."

"Everything will be all right now," you say. "Of that I'm certain."

You head to your chamber, and as you turn a corner you run into Prince Dastan.

"You may have won this round, Princess," he snarls, "but be warned. I will be keeping watch. You harm any of my family and I will make you pay."

You can tell by his ferocious expression that he means every word he says. You have made a powerful enemy. Yet you feel drawn to him—and his conviction.

You cannot let that worry you. Because the next thing you need to plan is your escape from the marriage.

But after how easily you retrieved the Dagger, you have no doubt you will find a way. Your role as a Guardian of the Dagger of Time has been tested, and you succeeded admirably in protecting it. You won't allow something as silly as a political marriage to keep you from your true destiny.

Not even a prince as handsome and courageous as Dastan.

THE END

No one notices you as you scurry out of the palace compound. If I were a prince, where would I spend my time? you wonder. Then bitterness stabs your heart. The correct question is: where would an invading Persian celebrate his cruel victory?

You push down your anger, mixed as it is with sorrow, and try to think. Often you've heard of soldiers celebrating in the taverns. Working men, too. If nothing else, there'd be talk. Dressed as one of them, the men may very well talk to you.

You rarely travel beyond the safety and comfort of the palace compound, other than on an occasional trip accompanied by guards. You feel a wave of excitement at being able to explore while unrecognized and virtually unseen. Then you remind yourself of your true task: *to protect the Dagger, no matter the consequences.*

You have heard of a district where there are many taverns as well as places for sport. You have only a vague notion of where it might be, but you set off, determined.

TURN TO PAGE 45

You trudge after him, your mind reeling with his revelation. Then you spot something odd up ahead. As you come closer, you realize the gruesome truth. Skeletons mounted on stakes dot the landscape. You and Dastan stop and stare at the sun-bleached bones.

"Who were these people?" you ask.

"Years ago, this valley held the biggest salt mine in the empire," Dastan tells you. "Until its slaves rose up. Killed their masters." He nods at the skeletons. "I heard they boiled them alive."

You try to hide your shudder. Dastan grins at you. "Welcome to the Valley of the Slaves," he says.

You enter the valley. Dastan leads Aksh through the cauldron of red sand, scanning for signs of trouble. You trail behind. Every fiber of your being is protesting. You do not want to take another step deeper into this dangerous territory.

You eye Dastan up ahead of you. Maybe you can bribe him for the Dagger. Or maybe you could pretend to faint, and when he comes to rescue you, you can steal it back.

Neither are foolproof plans. But you've got to do something before you go any further.

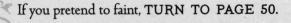

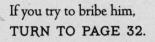

If you pretend to faint, **TURN TO PAGE 50.**

If you try to bribe him,
TURN TO PAGE 32.

"The dagger you wear in your belt," you announce.

You see you've surprised him. Well, what did he think you'd ask for? Pretty dresses? Jewelry? He doesn't know you at all.

But will he do it?

He holds your gaze a moment, clearly weighing his next move. But he truly can't deny you, not in front of his friends. Can he?

He pulls the dagger from his belt and examines it. You guess he's trying to understand why it's so important to you. You hold your breath.

Then he shrugs and holds it out to you. You take it from him, your hands trembling. You did it. You retrieved the Dagger!

Now you just have to get it safely out of the city and to its resting place in the temple found in the Hidden Valley. There is no time to lose! With a nod of thanks to Dastan, and before he can stop you, you race off. You need to find your horse, Astrella, and ride—fast!

TURN TO PAGE 40

You hear a moaning and feel tiny brushes across your face, tugs on your hair. "Stop!" you shout. "Who are you? What do you want?"

There's another lightning flash and your stomach tightens. There must be dozens of people! Some appear to have slit throats, others look ravaged by disease, some are very old; there are even some children who look as if they wasted away.

They look, you think with a shudder, dead. But that cannot be. . . .

"You are the one we've been waiting for," a disembodied voice says. It sounds like a chorus of echoes.

"What do you mean? What do you want me for?"

"We've been waiting so long," the voices moan. "You have what we need."

Now you feel tugs at your clothing, and it's clear from Astrella's behavior she feels them pawing through the saddlebags. In another lightning burst you realize the people are transparent. The truth hits you. You're surrounded by *ghosts*.

"What are you looking for?" you demand. "Who are you?"

"We are the ones who have always been here. But no one stays. No one helps us. We want to go back."

"Back where?" you ask. Where would ghosts be trying to go? And why would they think you could help them get there?

"Not where. *When!*"

Cold fear rises in you. Now you understand. They want the Dagger!

TURN TO PAGE 29

"I won't allow you to risk it," you insist. "This is my destiny—not yours."

Before he can say another word, you scurry to the cupola and down a winding staircase.

An earthquake shakes the walls, the floor. All is collapsing around you. You don't care—you have to stop Nizam.

He is approaching the Sandglass, his focus so intent that he doesn't even seem to be aware of the shaking and rumbling.

"Stop!" you cry. "Don't do it."

He turns and looks at you. And laughs. "You think you can stop me? A mere girl?"

That makes your blood boil. You charge at him. Then the ground rises up and cracks. This time the earthquake splits the floor!

Nizam stumbles, and as he desperately struggles to find something to hold on to, he stabs the Dagger into the Sandglass. The glimmering sand begins to flow. Pulled into it, you see time begin to rewind.

You go all the way back to . . .

TURN TO PAGE 11

"What is it you want to say to me?" he asks, clearly enjoying your shock.

"You have a dagger—it is sacred to my people. I want it back," you say. No sense denying it now that the ruse is up.

Dastan smirks at you. "Just like that. You ask, and I'm supposed to hand it over?" He pulls the Dagger from his belt and holds it up, turning it this way and that. The jewel catches the light, sending glinting rainbows across Dastan's face. "I kind of like it. And I won it in a fair fight."

Your heart sinks. "Asoka, my guard and advisor. Is he . . . Did you . . . ?"

"I won the fight, that's all. What happened to him after I left I have no control over."

"I should have taken the Dagger to safety myself," you murmur. "He should not have risked his life. That is *my* calling, *my* destiny." To your horror, tears begin to fall.

"I'm sorry, Princess Tamina," Dastan says, seeming genuinely concerned. "I didn't think my news would upset you. But it does make me wonder—what is so important about this weapon?"

This is exactly the question you've been hoping to avoid. You know that if he understood the Dagger's power, he would never give it to you. There's no choice—you're just going to have to take it!

You let out a shriek and fling yourself at the prince.

TURN TO PAGE 57

You are almost certain Dastan knows your true identity, and that makes you nervous. You would rather try your luck with his uncle, Nizam.

You just have to persuade Nizam that his nephew should return the Dagger.

"Please," you say, ducking your head to hide your face from them. "Allow me to speak to this kind gentleman alone. I—I don't feel I can speak sensibly in front of the young and handsome prince."

You want to choke on your own words, but your performance seems to have worked. Nizam chuckles and takes your arm.

"This way, young lady," Nizam says. "Now go, Dastan. Can't you see your charms are far too overpowering for such a simple girl?"

You bite the inside of your cheek to keep from retorting, but Dastan just looks at you quizzically, shrugs, then strolls away.

Nizam brings you to a marble bench. "Now what is it Dastan has that your mistress wants back, dear?" he asks kindly. "Her heart, perhaps? She'd rather marry Dastan—not Tus? And she wants me to intercede on her behalf?"

You fight back a laugh. How arrogant they all are. And how they underestimate you.

"No, sir," you say, speaking as meekly as you can. "She noticed that he has a certain . . . dagger."

TURN TO PAGE 75

One of the soldiers stands against the brick alley wall. There's a man beside Dastan—his manservant, you guess. Unlike Dastan, he looks concerned.

"You'll break your royal neck, sire," the man says.

"Bis, you worry too much," Dastan says. "I can do this."

You hover at the edge of the crowd, wondering what Dastan is planning. You see money exchanging hands—some sort of bet.

"Ready, Roham?" Dastan asks the man against the wall.

Roham grins. "Ready as I'll ever be. More to the point—are *you* ready?"

Dastan laughs. "As I'll ever be!"

He focuses on Roham. Then he charges straight at the man.

But instead of crashing into him, he runs beside him—right up the wall! One step! Two steps! Up and over Roham—then *wham!*

He falls.

The crowd bursts out laughing and applauding, Dastan laughing as hard as the rest of them.

"I told you, sire, it can't be done," Bis says.

"Maybe you're right," Dastan says. "Though I'd like to see the man who can do it. In fact, if *anyone* can, I'll give him anything he wants!"

You stifle a smile. Destiny continues to work in your favor.

"I can do it!" you declare.

TURN TO PAGE 92

Everyone freezes. The room grows silent, as all in it wait to hear what you have to say. You raise your chin proudly, keeping your expression neutral. You must stay clearheaded; emotion cannot rule you in this moment.

"Prince Tus," you say, forcing your gaze from the handsome man gripping your dagger. "Swear to me the people of Alamut will be treated with mercy."

Tus studies you a moment, then reaches out his hand again. Suppressing a shudder, you take it.

Nizam starts to applaud, and soon the rest of the chamber joins in. You force a smile. The applause means nothing. You are too focused on trying to figure out a way to get back your dagger.

TURN TO PAGE 81

"As my mistress's request is to the prince, I shall give the message to him and *only* him," you say, ducking your head.

"I'm sure you can say whatever it is you have to say in front of me as well," Nizam says.

Prince Dastan cocks his head and narrows his eyes. "No, I'll do as she wishes," he says to his uncle. Looking back at you, he adds, "You know the palace compound better than I do. Why don't you bring me somewhere where we can speak privately."

"Are you sure?" Nizam says. "Remember, this could be a ruse to do you harm. After all, the Alamutians *have* been making arms for your enemies."

"I think I can handle her," Prince Dastan says with a laugh. "Come."

You're about to protest his ordering you about, then remember your disguise. You drop a passable curtsy to Nizam and trip along beside Prince Dastan.

"In here," you say, gesturing to a small alcove off the plaza. "I'm sure we won't be overheard."

Prince Dastan steps into the enclosed space. "Good," he says. "Because I'm guessing you don't want anyone to know that Princess Tamina is skulking about dressed as her maid."

You gape at him. He knows!

TURN TO PAGE 122

The group charges you. You let out a shriek and race back into the twisting tunnels of the cave. Astrella gallops ahead of you.

The corridor and cave walls look different somehow. You're worried that you've taken a wrong turn somewhere. But you make it back to the cavern where you entered. You pick up the tiny box—only it seems bigger now. How is that possible?

At least the rain has stopped. You step out of the cave with Astrella. You know you can't stay a moment longer in that cave. Who knows how far the Dagger's effects can reach? You have to get away from here.

You climb onto Astrella, surprised that even though she's just a little filly, you still have a good seat in the saddle. You'd think your feet would nearly touch the ground. Can't worry about that now, you tell yourself. You have the Dagger to protect.

You ride a while and stop at a stream to drink. You bend over the clear water and notice your reflection.

You gasp. You've turned into a *child*! The cave looked different because you're shorter! The box looked bigger because your hands are smaller!

You grin. What a great disguise! No one will ever guess you're Princess Tamina, Guardian of the Dagger of Time! And once you place the Dagger in its sacred resting place, you will have a very long life to look forward to!

Yes, it will turn out all right in . . .

THE END.

You decide your best bet is for Kartosh to impersonate you. Watching the genie turn into you is very disconcerting. First he shrinks to your size, then his features shift and his clothing changes. Gone are the bracelets and the gold skin. What stands before you is your exact likeness. Even his mud horse resembles Astrella now.

"Go," he urges, "quickly. And no matter what, *don't look back*. They can track your fear. Move forward with conviction."

You nod and jangle Astrella's reins. You gallop away.

You hate not being able to turn around to see what's happening. But you must follow the rules Kartosh has set. You force your eyes forward.

After traveling for hours, it's no longer a struggle to believe in your success. Whoever was following you took the bait and went after Kartosh.

You arrive at the Guardian Temple unharmed. The Guardian priests greet you happily and take you to the temple where you put the Dagger away for safekeeping. You step outside and find Kartosh waiting beside the village well. He looks like his old self.

"They really don't grant wishes," he says, nodding at the well. "Not unless there's a wish-granting water genie inside."

"You're all right!" you exclaim. "I was so worried! And so grateful!"

"Then I'm sure you'll come up with an excellent reward for one so worthy as I!"

"I'm sure I will." You laugh. "Since I'm sure you'll tell me exactly what you want!"

THE END

"Princess Tamina," she greets you.

"You—you know my name?" you ask.

"I know all the Guardians of the Dagger of Time. Each generation. But you are the first who has had to make the journey north. Does this mean that Alamut is threatened?"

"Yes," you tell her sadly. "The Persians have invaded, and I fear it is the Dagger they seek."

She nods. "You have it with you, then?"

"Of course," you reply. Your fingers automatically finger the Dagger, hidden in your garments.

"Good," she says. "You may give it to me now."

This surprises you. Why would she want the Dagger? But she is the original Guardian—in a way, the Dagger is really hers.

You don't know what to do. You don't want to offend her, but it has been so ingrained in you never to give up the Dagger without knowing why.

If you think you should give it to her, TURN TO PAGE 30.

If it seems wrong to give her the Dagger,
TURN TO PAGE 37.

There is a small group of people standing beside the pool. They turn and wave at you. A young woman approaches you, smiling. "Welcome," she says in a melodious voice. "I am Chazika. If you found us and our little paradise, you must have been led here."

"I-I don't know," you say. "What is this place?"

She smiles at you. "We call it Eternal Springs, for time stands still here."

You stare at her. Can she be telling the truth? She radiates an otherwordly calm as she nods knowingly. "You don't believe me. I understand. But it's true. We've been here over one hundred years." She laughs at your shocked expression. "I know. I don't look that old, do I?"

She frowns and touches her temple, as if she had a headache. "I'm sorry. I suddenly feel a bit . . . dizzy."

Astrella whinnies beside you. You glance at her—then do a double take.

Instead of your powerful, steady mare, you're standing beside a young, excited filly!

TURN TO PAGE 94

Want the adventure to continue?
Find out what journeys Dastan goes on in:

TO RIGHT A WRONG

Written by Carla Jablonski
Based on the screenplay written by Doug Miro & Carlo Bernard
From a screen story by Jordan Mechner and Boaz Yakin
Executive Producers Mike Stenson, Chad Oman, John August, Jordan Mechner,
Patrick McCormick, Eric McLeod
Produced by Jerry Bruckheimer
Directed by Mike Newell

TURN THE PAGE FOR A SNEAK PEEK!

Prologue

Before the coming of the Prophet Mohammed, there was a harsh land that few could survive and none could control. But with the bold stroke of a sword and the sheer force of will, an empire rose from its rocky soil. That empire was Persia.

By the close of the sixth century, its reach extended from the beaches of the Mediterranean to the steppes of China. But like any empire, it was only as great as its princes—those who would one day be kings. . . .

Not all princes are born with royal blood. You, Prince Dastan, were found in the streets of Nasaf. You stepped in when one of the king's guards bullied another street urchin, your friend Yusef. King Sharaman admired your honesty, your courage, and your spirit. He saw great potential in you and adopted you into his family. The third and youngest of his sons.

That was twelve years ago. Now your father spends much of his time in prayer and contemplation. And your nation is on the verge of war.

 TURN TO PAGE 2

2

You pace in the war-council tent, just outside the beautiful city of Alamut. Although your father, the king, has clearly stated he wants the city spared, your older brothers—Tus, the heir to the kingdom, and Garsiv, the empire's military leader—along with your uncle Nizam, the king's brother, have decided to attack.

"But our father feels the city is sacred," you argue.

"The king doesn't know about this," Tus says.

"Then why . . . ?" you ask.

"Our finest spy intercepted a caravan leaving Alamut carrying these to our enemies in Koshkhan," Nizam says.

Tus gestures to a spy, standing by two trunks. The man tips them over, spilling weapons onto the ground. Your eyes widen. It's quite a lethal collection. It seems the rumors are true. The holy city of Alamut is not the peaceful place it claims to be. It is a center for making and selling weapons to your empire's enemies.

"We attack at dawn," Tus declares.

You disagree with the decision to fight—your father will be unhappy—but hold your tongue. Tus is in charge here. Still . . . you need to think about this.

Do you obey Tus's orders as a responsible young prince and command the rear battalion? Or do you come up with a plan of your own, possibly averting a bloodbath, but risking failure—and your family's wrath.

If you stick to your brother's plan, GO TO PAGE 74.

If you have a different idea,
CONTINUE ON TO PAGE 3.

3

It's now the middle of the night. You can hear the clamoring preparations for an attack on the city's main gate. With a small group of men, you sneak around to the eastern wall, a coil of rope and several grappling hooks slung over your shoulder.

You hear an Alamutian sentry pacing the parapet above you. You'll need to be very quiet. And fast.

You scale the wall as far as you can; then an arrow thunks between the stones above you. But this is no attack—this was planned between you and Bis, your manservant. More arrows pierce the wall, creating a ladder!

You use the arrows to climb the wall. When you're in position, you fling the grappling hook up and over the edge. It lands with a rather loud clunk.

Uh-oh.

The sentry must have heard it. His footsteps come closer. He peers over the side and looks right into your eyes. But before he can sound an alarm, a dagger flies from behind you and slams into him. He topples over the parapet. You send Bis a silent *thank you* as you climb over the wall. Then you drop the long rope to your commandos below.

"Remind me why we've disobeyed your brother's orders?" Bis says, panting as he struggles over the wall.

"Because a head-on attack will be a massacre. I'll need your shield."

"You know, sire," he says, handing it to you, "it appears to me you won't be happy till you get us all killed."

 TURN TO PAGE 27

You race across the courtyard to open the inner gate while your men work on the outer one. The guards must have heard because suddenly arrows rain down on you.

"Archers!" you shout. "Return fire!"

You reach the inner gate, carrying your own shield and wearing Bis's on your back. This is a critical moment. You get into position and hear a sizzling *whoosh* above you.

You lift your shield as boiling oil pours down on you. It bounces off your upraised shield—then it flows down the shield you're wearing on your back. Your plan worked!

You battle your way to the guard tower. You tip a vat of hot oil onto the street below, then grab a torch from its wall sconce. You fling the torch into the oil, sending up a wall of flame.

You rejoin Bis, and together you push open the outer gate. Your battalion roars into the city.

Dawn is just breaking now. This is when your brothers planned to attack. You've cleared a path for them. You climb onto a parapet to signal your brothers.

The battle begins in earnest.

 FIGHT YOUR WAY TO PAGE 5

5

At dawn, you are near the southern end of the walled city. Per Tus's orders, you will lead your commandos as backup for your brothers as they breach the main gates.

You wait anxiously for the signal. A wind is whipping up, and the horses are beginning to grow jumpy. You walk the ranks, giving encouragement.

Then you hear a sound you know and fear—the deep howl of a sandstorm. You turn to discover a dark wall of sand heading toward you.

There's nowhere to take cover! You can't wait for the command, you have to get inside the walled city. "Charge!" you shout as you race to get back to your horse, holding your sword high.

But it's too late. The sandstorm is upon you.

The horses whinny in fear and you sense confusion among the men. The sand pounds you, disorienting you, blinding you.

You have to find shelter, but this is unfamiliar terrain. You don't know which way to turn.

Suddenly, a voice says, "This way, Prince. I can get you to safety."

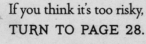 Do you follow the unseen stranger? TURN TO PAGE 69.

 If you think it's too risky,
TURN TO PAGE 28.